Storyteller Journal of Writing and the Arts

Started in 2017

Volume 7 · Issue 11 · September 2023

ISBN: 978-1-955783-11-8

EDITOR
Shay Shivecharan

COPY EDITOR
Michael Birk

ASSOCIATE EDITORS
Gabriel McLeod, Joshua Mahn

COVER PHOTOGRAPHY
Jeannie Albers

FEATURED ON COVER
Alex Gurtis, Aaron Morrison, Gabriel McLeod, Joshua Mahn, Lisa Bui, Londyn Rayne, Nicholas Michael Reeves, Shay Shivecharan

 threeowlspublishing.com/storytellerjournal

 storyteller@threeowlspublishing.com

 fb.com/storytellerjournal

 @storytellerjournal

---

Storyteller is a publication of **Three Owls Publishing**

THREE OWLS
PUBLISHING

JEANNIE ALBERS

Art Director & Photographer

JEANNIEALBERS.COM

CONTRIBUTORS

Aaron Morrison

Aaron was born during the great __natural disaster__ in the _season_ of _year_. He spends his free time exploring __unusual location__ and raising domesticated __fictional creature(plural)__. One day, he would like to _verb_ his way to _place_ and try the various _noun(plural)_.

@theaaronmorrison

linktr.ee/TheAaronMorrison

Blake Slaughter

Blake Slaughter, born and raised in Central Florida, has been writing since he was 11 years old. From songs, to stories, to poetry, Blake has had an intense passion for creating the fictional worlds that reside in his head and doesn't plan to put the pen down anytime soon. He attributes most of his inspiration to his exposure to horror and drama pieces at a young age, and to classic music.

@blakeeslaughter

Alex Gurtis

Alex Gurtis is a poet and critic whose work has appeared or is forthcoming in *Autofocus*, *The Shore*, *HAD*, *Rejection Letters*, *Saw Palm* and others. A ruth weiss foundation Maverick Poet Award Finalist, Alex received his MFA from the University of Central Florida and is the co-owner of the independent bookstore, Zeppelin Books.

@apbg_alex

Lily Perez

Hello everyone! My name is Lily Perez. I am 20 years old, I enjoy creative writing, reading, doing puzzles, taking care of my plants, and being a wife and a mother to my husband Casey and daughter Salem. Getting coffee or thrifting with a friend is how I like to spend time with people I care about.

@lilyeliza25

Emma Guernsey

Emma is an amateur photographer from Central Florida hoping to share glimpses of the world through scenes captured and stories collected on her journeys. Though American by birth, she is a citizen of the world, and seeks to understand the fullness of that heritage.

 @eggieraw

www.etsy.com/shop/PhotosByEggie

Londyn Rayne

Londyn Rayne is a poet, songwriter and spoken word artist. Often blending words rich in both melancholy and hope, accompanied by a cinematic soundscape for the message to rest in. Bending back and forth between melody and poetry, creativity is her most comfortable form of communication and she uses it to advocate for emotional and mental health and healing. Her debut poetry collection *Smokescreen* is available now through Three Owls Publishing.

 @londynrayne

Vanessa Frances

Vanessa Frances is the author of three poetry collections, written through her teenage and young adult life. She holds a BA in Digital Journalism and Media from Pennsylvania State University and is pursuing an MS in Environmental Law from Vermont Law and Graduate School. She works as a marketer, managing editor, musician, and dog walker.

 @faaemusic

Lisa Bui

Lisa is currently pursuing her Computer Science degree at UCF. She loves to visit coffee shops and journal, as well as going on foodie adventures around town with her friends. On her nights in, Lisa loves to watch a good crime show. Her favorites are Criminal Minds, Law & Order SUV, and Suits.

@lisaaabuiii

CONTRIBUTORS

Gabriel McLeod

Gabriel is an artist and writer that hails from the Deep South and currently resides in a moment of time at a corner of Earth known as Florida. He found meaning through the escape in creativity at an early age and has been chasing that feeling ever since. He is honored to be part of the *Storyteller* family.

@gabrielmcleod

Darryl Pickett

Darryl Pickett is a former Walt Disney Imagineer and theme park consultant. He left Winter Garden in 2020 to rejoin family in Albuquerque, New Mexico. He began writing *The Bonnie and Clyde Death Car* 10 years ago, and completed it for this relaunch edition of *Storyteller*.

@flippyshark

Nicholas Michael Reeves

Raconteur. Crossword maven. Writer of *Letters to the Dead*. An aspirant Warhol of the poem. I love the taste of words. Taste, for instance, *a fogged window, an abandoned railroad, a lone crow, coffee-stained postcards*. Then ask the question: Where would civilization be if we didn't write about them? Then take a deep breath. I'm no hero or anything. Someone has to translate the birdsong, interpret the silence, and eavesdrop on you—stranger. eavesdrop on you—stranger.

@nicholasmichaelreeves

Joshua Mahn

Joshua Mahn learned to write by scrying through an obsidian mirror. Shortly after this, he learned to speak. His favorite novel is a pile of bones he stacked in the swamp, and he asks your help in ensuring it stays hidden, lest the ancient magics dissipate. Most days, he can be found beneath your floorboards, if he's not in your attic.

@joshmahnwrites

Gabrielle Roessler

Gabrielle is a creative sprinter – she writes short stories, poetry, and creative nonfiction that prove she made great returns on her therapy investments. Her work has been featured in *The Winnow, Hallowzine, Journal of Erato, Warning Lines, The Midnight Mass Anthology,* and elsewhere. When she isn't having an existential crisis through her MFA, she enjoys traveling with her fiancé and adding more stamps to their National Parks passport.

@hobbituallygabby

Storyteller is always looking for new voices and fresh perspectives. Submissions can be made to: **storytellersubmissions@gmail.com**

Dear Emily Elizabeth Dickinson

by Nicholas Michael Reeves

Dear Emily Elizabeth Dickinson,

"Open me carefully."

"I am nobody! Who are you?"
Oh Emily.

I am a nobody,
a nobody too.

I do not know much
about you—because you
wanted it that way—

but I know more than
I should, thanks to Lavinia.

Your raspy deathbed wish:
destroy all my letters, sister.

But you said nothing of
poems she unearthed.

Pulses of your heart, as
you deemed those lines
that broke mine,

eighteen hundred of them beating on motley scraps—
chocolate wrappers, newspaper
clippings, letters themselves.

Years ago I made my pilgrimage
to Amherst, licking my lips for
that line of yours—

"earth is crammed with heaven,
but poetry is a house that
tries to be haunted."

It began to make sense,
why at the station they warned
me to steer far from 280 Main Street
because the house indeed is haunted.

The Myth who lives there might
be a ghost, they said.

She hasn't left the house
in two decades—and
she hides in the closet when
the doorbell rings.

If she does answer,
it's only in the dark.

I was only there to leave
you a letter, your preferred
method of communication,

hoping you
might find it ambling
out to your rose garden.

Because the only commandment
you ever obeyed was to consider the lilies,
I pressed one in the paper,
white as the dresses you wore.

A bit more subtle than my
colleague Billy, who in the year 1998,
wrote a poem about taking your clothes off,

from your tulle tippet to your
pearl buttons, all the way down to the
complex infrastructure of your nineteenth
century undergarments.

Needless to say, I'm
not trying to hold a séance
to get into your corset.

I only wanted to tell you—
they don't rhyme like you
anymore, Emily.

Seamless, silken rhymes,
akin to the rhyme of the
wind and the birds and the sky.

Read enough Dickinson
your world starts to sing.

You are everywhere to me.

Now my precious
morns are metered,

I eye the couplet
of the coffee and the spoon

and wait for the rhyme
of rain on the tin roof.

Once in the Boston Harbor
I saw the ocean and moon
trying to compose one of yours.

Imitation is suicide,
I told them. Go back to bed.

Then came this morning
when I broke my golden rule—

never to write before the

birds start singing.

(I'm a translator, after all.)

But dawn woke me

in her white house dress,

honey on her lips

to kiss the dark good-bye.

I decided I'd write her another letter.

How beautiful were those

streams of pollen that rolled

down her flushed cheeks.

How glad I am

Lavinia found her

hidden in the cherrywood.

Like all poets, I pointed

the flashlight of the pen

in my direction,

where I began

to wonder if one day

someone would find me.

But supposedly I take after my

Goldfish—supposedly—

and all I know now is this.

I don't want to forget me.

If I have forgotten me, how
won't the world?

Lately I've been placing
hands into my wounds, wondering,
am I true?

To look back on a life and see:
We want to forget our pain,
and yet be known for having
survived it.

So now I reach for my memories
like lamp chains in the dark.

Because you taught me to look
at words, Emily, until they shine.

We can't be the only people in the
world who see the word *honey* like I do,
can we?

Some sixty-watt bulb in an attic of
yesterdays.

Honey. Glowing like

that summer day in 1987

when I floated

through the rolling

daffodil hills

and the honeybees

answered the call of

the flowers

and I swore I saw

you in one of them.

Honey. Maybe it's the sun

drooling down the side

of the barn that day,

or the rust of

the old station wagon

sunk into the field.

Or maybe *honey* is a day

I dog-eared long ago

in the little book of my life.

I don't know, Emily,

I never was a writer in

any sense of the word except

I love the way words taste.

And I love the clasp
of the mailbox
and the stain of coffee
on an old piece of stationary,

and I love knowing
I let go a piece of me
into this world not so
lost I cannot be found again,

even if death has
taken me through the woods
on that coal black train

and there is no one
else to translate the birdsong.

BACK WHEN THERE WERE MORE OF US

BY AARON MORRISON

The swamp now encompasses our town.

Menacing cypress trees wall us in and the dangling Spanish moss sways like hungry tentacles.

Pete Diaz ventures into the muck and says he'll return with help.

Shotgun gripped tight, he wades into the swamp, until the murky green reaches midway up his shins.

He passes by the angry cypress knees and disappears from sight as the trees swallow him up.

We hear the thunder from his shotgun, followed by Pete Diaz screaming a scream no one should make...

We now know that there are worse things than gators in the swamp.

ROOTS
BY VANESSA POULSON

Cleo loved her tomato plant

She stored it on the top shelf of her bathroom, where the humidity was plentiful, and the corners of its leaves could reach up against the glass towards the sunlight. The plant was just two months old but had already given her five, plump cherry tomatoes. Each of them a delightful deep red, bursting on her teeth and filling the inside of her mouth with seeds.

The only thing Cleo liked nearly as much as tomatoes were strawberries. She wasn't sure why though, maybe it was something about the color red.

Today was Saturday, and the humidity was overflowing Cleo's bathroom with dense heat. Cleo was trying to tame her unruly mane of hair, picking knots out of her matted, graying blonde hair.

It was important for her to look her best today, she thought, smudging brown eyeshadow across her eyelids.

For the first time in a month, Cleo had plans today. She had a date.

The date was tonight at seven, at a restaurant just a few miles from her house. It looked like a really nice place, according to the photos she'd pulled up on Google: tall white columns, huge open windows, and real wooden floors.

She couldn't believe in all the years she'd lived here that she'd never seen this place before. Had she known about it, she'd have begged a number of past suitors to take her through the solid wood doors, showing her off on their arm to the other patrons.

Nevertheless, Cleo was excited.

After reading the menu online, she knew that the restaurant served seafood, and Cleo had written down what she might like to order in a notebook she'd slid into the pale green purse she was planning on wearing tonight. The problem was, she didn't have a single dress to match.

Deciding that wouldn't be a problem, Cleo swung open the bathroom door back into her bedroom, nearly tripping on the boxes scattered all over the floor. She'd find a dress, one made to make the whole restaurant notice.

In her excitement for this evening, Cleo had strewn clothes all around the room looking for something to match the green purse. The fabric of multiple skirts and dresses clumped themselves into canyons across the landscape of her bedroom, casting the tight space in a kaleidoscope of color. Still, none of them fit the image she had in her head of what she wanted to look like tonight.

Marching back through the discarded fabric, Cleo felt her foot brush against something heavy on the floor. Looking down, Cleo discovered she'd knocked over her bookshelf last night in the frenzy. It had gotten lost underneath the eighth wonder of the world she'd carved out of her bedroom, the bottom wooden corner just barely visible from underneath an array of fabric.

Carefully, she bent over and lifted the heavy bookshelf onto the top of her back, pushing it up against the wall until it was fully upright. Only a few books had been casualties in the frenzy, while the rest had managed to hold on to the shelf. An aged copy of *Galapagos* by Kurt Vonnegut and a new-age book of medicine that she'd borrowed from a bookstore down the road yesterday were both flipped onto their backs on the floor.

Cleo had almost entirely forgotten about that trip, remembering only being in the store for a moment, then the next having arrived back home, the book buried deep in the green purse. She was entirely unsure how she'd gotten it, but placed both books back on the top shelf.

If there was nothing here for her to wear, she decided she'd better get out and go somewhere that might have something suitable.

She piled her hair on top of her head in a heavy ponytail and gathered what she needed to take with her to the clothing store to find a dress. After finding her chapstick under a navy blue skirt, her wallet behind a ripped blanket, and her sequined belt, she paced back and forth within the room twice before reaching for the door handle.

Before she stepped out into the hallway, she looked behind her towards the bathroom, where the tomato plant sat in the bathroom window, its small green leaves lifted as if waving her goodbye.

"Oh alright," she sighed, stepping back into the bathroom and picking the tomato plant up by the pot. "I guess you can come with me."

Cleo couldn't remember the last time she'd driven anywhere, so her journey to the clothing store would be by bicycle.

Carefully, she flung the green purse over her shoulder, making sure it was well out of the way of slipping off her shoulder and getting caught on the bicycle gears and placed the tomato plant in the cupholder on the handlebars. Cleo twisted the tomato plant into place in the cupholder, making sure it was secure, before pushing up the kickstand and starting down the road.

She wasn't sure why she knew this, but there was a clothing store that wasn't too expensive just around the corner from where she was living.

Since it was a Saturday morning, the roads were quiet, and Cleo biked lazily on the road, listening for cars but hearing none. Though it was warm, there was still an unmistakable breeze, which pulled her hair out from its ponytail and sent it in streamers down her back.

The wind reminded her of the Bahamas, where she'd lived for several years. After becoming discouraged in America, fed up with college and the constant feeling of being rushed everywhere, she decided she'd find somewhere else to call home.

Cleo worked at a snorkeling business on the island of Bimini, convincing the woman that ran it that she could learn quickly. She spent her days swimming, working with tourists, and teaching them how to snorkel. Bimini was famous for a shipwreck off its coast, and Cleo led daily tours to it. Tourists were excited to have someone familiar, an American woman, show them around the Caribbean island. Not that she was an expert on Bimini or anything related to snorkeling, but she was exceptional at getting tourists to give her money.

She had met several people in Bimini, including the father of her daughter. Living in Bimini felt like a daydream, every part of reality oversaturated with bliss to the point it all felt completely surreal. There was no one breathing down her neck telling her how to live her life. There was always something new and exciting to do. There wasn't anything that felt boring or mundane.

She liked that, a lot.

When she'd left Bimini with her daughter, for several reasons she couldn't remember, she'd lost touch with most of her friends and her daughter's father. She wasn't sure where he was now, and for the most part, she wasn't concerned. Although, sometimes when she'd spent most of the day alone, letting her thoughts wander, she'd imagine herself still living on the island and raising their daughter by the ocean instead of living alone in the swamp.

A pickup truck sped out of the neighborhood and around the bend of the road, sending Cleo swerving out into the bike lane. The truck roared its engine, racing through the yellow light and ahead on the road, ignoring Cleo completely.

She heard an intense, loud noise in the distance, impossible forces colliding together and echoing throughout the space surrounding it, and she flinched. Cleo looked backward for a moment, hesitating. She could have broken a bone if she hadn't been paying attention, but luckily, Cleo had survived much worse than that.

Besides, she had a dress to find.

Catching her breath, she reached out, feeling the cupholder, her hands racing along all parts of the tomato plant, looking for bumps and bruises, broken stems, or torn leaves. Luckily, the tomato plant had survived her evasive maneuver. She cupped the base of the plant's stem between her fingers, leaning down and planting a single kiss on the side of it.

"You're safe, don't you worry."

> **" When they asked her why she'd left, however, those lies were much harder to spin.**

She kicked back onto the bike, continuing her journey down the sidewalk, this time a bit more cautious.

Shortly after, Cleo reached one of the busiest intersections in their small city and rolled the bike up to a scurried halt beside the pedestrian walk button. The stream of cars was steady here, the faucet of the weekend traffic at full force. Cleo placed her hand firmly on the handlebars, steadying the tomato plant against the racing wind coming out of traffic as it waved back and forth with the passing cars.

The walk sign turned white, and Cleo kicked off her bike and set out through the crosswalk, turning and looking over both of her shoulders over and over again. She would not be surprised by another car, no way.

The sun was bright, and Cleo could feel her exposed shoulders prickling in the heat. It was so much warmer than she remembered it being as a child, the weight of the weather making this familiar route seem longer than ever.

Along with the intensified heat, the whole city had hit a growth spurt in her absence. When she'd returned, the buildings were taller, the once quiet streets had become dense with people. The city was fuller, with new titan skyscrapers and main roads bulldozed through former sidestreets.

There were moments when Cleo felt like a stranger here, most of which she ignored, but there were times she found herself severed from the reality around her, floating in a place that no longer existed.

One of the nice parts about moving back to your hometown was that there were people that knew you from before you left that had stayed behind. To them, you were still the exciting person that decided to leave in the first place.

Cleo had left town an adventurer, hero, and returned, an icon. She'd explored the world and lived somewhere people here had only seen in coffee table books or in television documentaries. When she'd run into groups of people she knew before she'd moved, her time in Bimini could be anything she wanted it to be. She'd been a professional skydiver to some of them. A bed and breakfast owner to others. To others still, she'd been the wife of a millionaire, responsible for the largest housing development in all of Bimini.

When they asked her why she'd left, however, those lies were much harder to spin.

"Oh, he was a *monster*," she'd always tell people, lowering her voice and softening her expression. "It was best I took our daughter away, back to the safety of the States."

Cleo felt better as their faces softened in sympathy with her story, and though made up, she was safe in their knowing expressions. They'd take her hand and tell her how brave she was for knowing she had to leave, even if it made her sad. They'd remind her that everyone here supported her, and loved her, no matter what.

People loved feeling as if they'd been let in on a secret, and it didn't matter if it was true or not. It was the feeling it gave them that counted. Cleo knew she could leverage that to her advantage.

Finally across the street, Cleo looked up at the fluorescent sign of the clothing store, an open sign blinking on and off in the window. She parked her bike on the outer part of the sidewalk walkway, looking down at the tomato plant.

"Do you want to stay out here?" she asked, rubbing one of the leaves between her fingertips. She waited gingerly, stroking the top of the stem.

"Oh alright, I guess you can come in with me. It'll be good to get your opinion."

The front door of the store was heavy and sighed as Cleo pried it open. In her left hand, she held the tomato plant, running her thumb gently down one of the leaves. The AC from inside brushed the leaf back against her finger, crossing them one over top of the other.

There were a lot of young people in the store, scattered around the different sections of shirts and pants, everything color coated in streamlined aisles.

Cleo meandered over to the dresses, finding her size and grinning to find how many different shades of green dresses there were. She took the purse off from over her shoulder and held the bag up to each and every dress in the section, looking for the perfect match.

"Do you need help finding anything?" A sweet, cheery voice called from behind her, over the sounds of metal hangers clinking across the racks.

"No, I think I'm just fine, thanks," Cleo answered, her attention drawn back to the hundreds of green dresses, glazing her finger over the top of them as she meandered through the aisle.

"What do you think of this one?" she whispered to the tomato plant. "Surely it's a bit too dark for me."

The tomato plant almost lifted its leaves up in a shrug.

"Maybe it's worth trying on."

Cleo pulled the dress off the rack, turning forward to walk down the rest of the aisle.

"Mom?"

The same cheery voice returned, this time in a hurried whisper from over her shoulder. A hand appeared on her wrist, small and slight like her own, pulling on her hand wrapped tight around the tomato plant.

"Excuse me, you're going to hurt him," she urged, almost hissing, jerking her hand back from the girl. "Don't you see he's still little?"

Her hand retreated, the girl looked back at Cleo, with deep amber eyes and tight curls tumbling over her shoulders.

Cleo met the eyes of her near doppelganger's eyes only after recognizing the cool white striped scar on the top of her forearm.

She would know that scar anywhere, no matter what. There was no reframing something that never faded, no hometown reunion for something so permanent.

It had been a heated exchange between two adults, a baby shoved into the sharp frame of a window. It was a scar Cleo had to explain to teachers, to friends, and to herself, no matter what she did to try and forget. It was an accident, but one she was responsible for.

"Lea?"

Lea frowned, biting down on her lip.

"Mom, what are you doing here?"

"I- I needed a dress. I have a date tonight." Cleo stumbled, feeling flustered, her heart thumping in her chest.

Lea crossed her arms across her chest, eyes flickering between the tomato plant, the green purse, and her mother.

Cleo, suddenly self-conscious, used her free hand to brush some of the dirt off her unwashed pants. She looked smaller standing next to her daughter, who had her father's tall stature, but Cleo's narrow bones. Lea looked so much older, her stone-faced, but her eyes gave away the childlike fear in her expression.

"I asked you not to come to where I work, do you remember that?" Lea lowers her voice to match her gaze. "You're going to get me in trouble if you don't leave."

Cleo's hands fumbled around the dress hanger. Is that why she remembered there was a clothing store nearby? Because Lea worked here? Or because Lea had told her specifically *not* to come?

Cleo stood back, suddenly offended. "Your boss would just throw out a paying customer?"

"Can you *please* leave?"

"No. No, I won't." Cleo's hand tightens around the tomato plant, pulling it close to her body. "I haven't done anything wrong, I'm here to buy a dress."

Lea stepped further into Cleo's row, her hip brushing through all the green dresses until she was inches from Cleo.

"Have you been drinking?" she asked.

"Lea, you know I haven't had a *single* sip since before I got pregnant."

Lea frowned. "Mom, you promised."

The strength in her expression wavered. "I... I can't stand to see you like this anymore. We talked about this..."

Cleo held tightly to the tomato plant, her grip pushing some of the soil up to the brim of the pot and sprinkling it down onto the carpet. Lea's eyes followed the brown flurries all the way to the floor, lips pressed tightly together.

Lea's eyes flipped to the tomato plant in Cleo's clenched hand, and to Cleo's eyes; disheveled, bloodshot, and exhausted. Lea traced the lines of Cleo's face, her gaze catching the distortion around Cleo's nose, the skin around the outside sagging and inflamed. She looked sicker than ever, worse than when she'd got out of the hospital just two weeks before.

Watching as Lea took her in, Cleo's eyes hurried around the store, looking for the exit. The door was miles away from the green dresses. With shaking hands, Cleo droped the green purse, wrapping both her hands tightly around the tomato plant frantically.

"It's okay," she whispers, her voice jumping up the octave, kissing the top of each and every leaf. "No one's hurting you. No one. You're safe right here with me."

"Mom, let's-"

Lea reached for Cleo, but Cleo pulled her arm away, bending down to pick up the purse from the floor and flinging it back over her shoulder. There was fear across Lea's face now, all strength deteriorating as Cleo's emotions intensified.

"Do I need to call-?"

"I think we best be going," Cleo's voice constricted over her forced grin, teeth clenched. Control.

"Thank you for your help."

Cleo stormed towards the door, pushing back open the heavy door and running towards her bike. Lea raced behind her all the way to the front door, lips poised open as if to shout, before her mouth collapsed shut, and let the door close between them.

There were tears in Cleo's eyes, but she didn't remember wanting to cry. She never cried, at least, not without deciding to do so first.

Struggling, Cleo forced the tomato plant back into the cupholder, confused as to how it suddenly had become too big for the same container she brought it here in. She shoved it down into the cupholder harder, more soil lost to the sidewalk.

"It's just a green dress," Cleo murmurs under her breath, ignoring the cautionary tale of the blinking red hand and racing across the intersection. "I've gotten myself into a tizzy over a *little green dress.*"

Cleo took the path off of the road the whole way this time, her hearing muffled, turning the whole world into a softened version of itself. Her vision remained blurry and inconsistent as she followed the cracks in the sidewalk back to her home, the tightness in her chest made her forget the word that she once used for this place.

Without realizing it, she'd left the front door open, the inside warm and muddy with humidity. There wasn't any furniture in this room, only cardboard, and scattered cushions with no structures to hold them. Was this her place as she'd imagined it? She felt unsure, now that everything was both clearer and more dissonant than before.

Looking up, Cleo realized the walls were sinking down with the weight of the air, creating depressions against her shoulder as she slammed into the inside, attempting to push them up and out of her way. They were persistent, the room was too tight and would not be moved. There was no way of reconstructing it.

This space no longer looked right, but raggedy and outdated, with flies pooling across the walls and mismatched and broken wood across the floor.

Was this really where she lived?

Cleo crawled up to her room, finding her clothes in their same disheveled state. At least this much was true. She threw the green purse down against the floor, scrambling her hands across each panel of fabric and holding them up to the skylight, none of them green, none of them quite right.

"Do you think this matches?" Cleo asks the tomato plant, still clutched in her hand, frantic and uncoordinated. "What about this one?"

Falling to her knees, Cleo continued digging through the fabric, launching one thing after another back up into the air, revealing the lump of her family heirlooms concealed below her closet expedition, photos of her life in Bimini, Lea's second-grade class photo, and an expired rental ticket for diving gear. Cleo swept her hands through the floor's treasures, all her life's possessions of various shades and ages, turning up relics, but nothing green.

Cleo's phone rang, but she couldn't find it in the new mess she'd made. The vibration of the phone rattled underneath some impossible mass on the floor, Cleo reached around the canyons and buried her hands all the way to the carpet, still coming up with everything besides the thing she was looking for. The room was too tight, constricting, smaller and smaller until there was almost no more space for Cleo or anything else.

The vibrating stopped.

There were birds singing soft songs outside the window, almost like she was back on the island. Cleo hurried to the bathroom, hoping to catch a glimpse of them through her small window. She spied one in the tree just across from the way. It was bouncing along one of the branches, stopping only when it was perfectly eye-to-eye with her.

Its feathers were the perfect shade of green.

"Do you see that?" Cleo called, running back to the bedroom and picking up the tomato plant. There were indents on its small container where her hands had constricted around it, the plant crooked and uneasy, nearly falling out of the crushed pot.

"That bird is just the perfect thing, don't you think?" Cleo ran her fingers back over the leaves of the tomato plant, propping it back up in the bathroom window. The bird looked over, suddenly curious.

"Do you want to see it better?" Cleo asked the tomato plant. "Here, watch this," she lowered her voice, sharing yet another secret. "I know the best way to bird watch."

She scurried back into her room and found the bag of birdseed at the bottom of her bookshelf, realizing its weight had knocked the bookshelf over to begin with. Tearing into the bag, Cleo brought a fist full of seed with her back into the bathroom, sprinkling it all over the windowsill.

"Now you'll get to see it up nice and close."

Cleo pulled the window open, and after a moment of tender curiosity, the green feathered bird soared over, landing in the window and scavenging through the seed. Cleo squealed with delight, the bird hopped from seed to seed, quickly clearing the windowsill until it stood face-to-face with the tomato plant.

The bird cocked its head, eyes black, beady, and directionless, sprung its body forward, and pulled a tomato from the plant, leaving a slash across the stem.

"Hey!" Cleo shouted, eyes ripe with panic, trying to shoo the bird away. "Don't do that!"

The bird didn't answer but took another tomato.

"That's it," Cleo shouted, pulling the window down at full force, knocking the tomato plant out of the frame and towards the earth below. The bird stared at her blankly, before diving down to the earth below landing beside the plant. It looked back up at Cleo just for a moment, before continuing to eat.

"No!" Cleo's voice broke.

"Come back!"

The tomato plant didn't respond.

"Can't you hear me?" she shouted. "Get up! GET UP!"

Cleo turned around and brushed towards the door of the bathroom, stumbling back through her messy bedroom. She'd get that bird. She'd *kill* that bird for what it had done.

Just as she reached for the door, in the corner of her eye, she spied it. Hidden beside a pair of cracked diving goggles and behind a binder stuffed with her discharge papers was a green dress.

Grinning, she reached down, holding the garment up to the skylight. She couldn't believe she nearly missed it, almost having lost it in her frantic upheaval of the room.

It was perfect, exactly what she was looking for.

Cleo brushed her hands down the smooth fabric. It was so shiny, she could see her own reflection staring back at her. She looked beautiful against the green, it complemented her skin so well.

It was made for her. It had to have been.

Without a second thought, she held the dress tight to her body and stepped back into the bathroom to try it on.

THE PRECISION

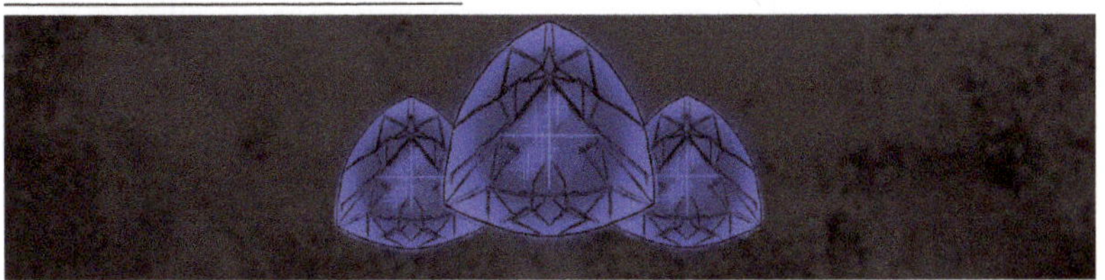

BY AARON MORRISON

Derek Terpin smirks as a heavy raindrop slaps and shatters against the windshield of his parked car.

The predicted weather will explain the sudden power outage to come, and will delay emergency response by one minute and forty seven seconds.

He adjusts his tie, exits the car, bounds up the museum steps, and steps through the doors.

The full force of the storm crashes down behind him.

Bethany Alverez, Derek's mark and lover of four months, smiles and leads him to the vault for a private viewing of the Nightstar Sapphires.

Derek sees, but does not acknowledge, Amanda Cross perusing exhibits, ready to text Wilheim Davis to cut the power and, if needed, cause a distraction to aid in Derek's exit.

In the vault, Derek counts down to zero in his head.

The power goes off, and, in the dark, Derek switches out replicas for the real deal, with one second to spare as the generator kicks on.

Mission complete, Derek smirks as he exits the museum.

His right foot on the first step down slips on slick algae, and he cracks his head on hard concrete.

Derek Terpin dies one minute and forty seven seconds before the ambulance arrives.

PERIHELION
(Precursor to Spring)

by Gabriel McLeod

Winter washes weary

water colored remains of the months that have past

Cords and blinking lights drip from dying branches

Tinsel twinkled litter box, brown pine needles lead path

To the back yard where the

Frost murdered but melted

Birds of Paradise tremble

Black and crackling

Like the mummified skulls of Crows

Swaying in the unusually cold breeze

Awaiting the rebirth of Spring

The chorus in their refrain rings, rustle, hustle, rustle

This dawning of the new season brings a sublime dismal sadness

Sparkling speckled with hope

My soul is naturally nocturnal but my heart is heliotropic

While winter washes wearily away

I can already tell the onslaught frothing green has begun unseen

This frigid darkness is striped with warm possibility

This divine madness sparkles with jewels yet to be discovered

When this Winter closes its page

I will, like the Jasmine, like the Marigold and Magnolia,

like the Song of Birds and Cicadas and Frogs

I will Sing in Color, will Blossom in Sound

Will rise up above this cold damp memory of the past

And rise and rise and rise brighter and warmer than before

Can you feel it?

We are closer to the light than we have ever been

One more time again

Leaves in the Tops of Trees

by Gabriel McLeod

The leaves in the tops of the trees,

whisper secrets in the breeze.

If you bend down low and listen,

you will hear.

The stars are marbles in a black and blue velvet bag,

waiting between wonder and play.

The Cheshire sliver of moon

is a crooked smile from an old friend,

that knows the secret joke

only we share.

We were born giants

But we've trained ourselves to be smaller,

 to match the physical and mental statures of those we are around.

To lean and crouch and be crooked

to lower our voice and limit our words

to hide our stories and colors

to dim our shine.

There are nights, where the dark is just right

to stretch to your full height

and our howls don't have to be alone.

Somewhere out there, others are howling too.

Stretch with me, grow with me,

 embrace the beautiful weird we can be.

The leaves in the tops of the trees

Whisper secrets in the breeze

If you bend down low and listen

You will hear.

hide & seek

by Londyn Rayne

Do not disturb
I may not speak
or hurt out loud.
I weep in secret,
like the moon when it sinks—
cowering behind a comforting cloud.
But if my silence
is something you're able to hear
as a familiar sound,
please stay.
Forgive me.
I'm healing from stories
no one knows except for me.
Sometimes crying is all i can say,
but if my tears are able to communicate
clearly to you,
please stay.

Tethered by knots
so whether i'm ready or not,
awaken me
from my temporary static
instigated by dormant pain.
Inspire me like the heat
in the blue part of a flame,
and should i get scared again
I promise I won't push you away.
You found me in my hiding place.
Please stay.

Storyteller

Past, Present, and Future

Letter from the Editor

We are here to create stories. This is our best destiny and our greatest purpose. It is what we're born for, and what ultimately defines our legacy. How we are remembered, in the hearts of loved ones, in the minds of friends and colleagues, perhaps in the annals of history, hinges on what these stories are, and how deeply we live them.

We are here to tell stories, it is our nature to do so. We talk, we write. We draw, we paint. We capture moments in time. We dance and we sing.

We imagine and we dream. We live for those dreams. We are the creators of worlds unseen, never before conceived.

We search for meaning in this life, while giving meaning to that very search through the stories we create, and the ones we are brave enough to tell.

We are the ones that remember, the ones generations to come won't forget.

The beautiful group pictured, captured so magnificently by the talented Jeannie Albers (who has now shot seven of our covers), consists of authors who have been a big part of our first ten issues. These individuals, along with a few others who could not join us for the shoot, have been the heart and soul of Storyteller's past. I'm also certain they will factor largely in its future. I can't say enough how important their contributions have been to this project over the years.

Storyteller began in 2017, an effort born of discontent and frustration. Unpublished writers all too often struggle to find their footing in a craft that initially presents them few opportunities, if any, for showcasing their talent and effort. If lucky, they may find a friend on the same journey to exchange stories with, or maybe family members willing to volunteer as tribute (and read their work), hoping for any morsel of encouragement or feedback, a reason to stick with it. Before it had a name, Storyteller had its mission- to create a printed medium through which aspiring writers in the West Orlando community could have their stories and poems finally published in a format that carried a professional look and feel.

Having grown up with countless volumes of Readers Digest and National Geographic magazines at my disposal (thanks Mom and Dad), I was inspired to create something worthy of these longstanding, iconic publications. By the third issue, I brought a dear and gifted friend named Lydia aboard as editor. The mission was evolving; we not only wanted to provide

---

a platform, we became committed to helping each of our writers find their best voice, without changing what they had to say.

In August of 2021, we published our tenth issue. More notably, we had continued to evolve the publication in small but important ways, including holding regular contests with cash prizes. And yet while we continued to grow, the train was slowing down by the middle of 2022. Someone in the publishing business once told me how hard it would be to continue, to find the funds, the time, and the energy to carry on over the years. I had finally reached that point and Storyteller went on indefinite hiatus.

Many years ago, my mother taught me a valuable lesson when she told me, "Where there is a will, there is a way." I never gave up on Storyteller, I still had the will, even if the way had become difficult to navigate.

A few months ago, by way of a rather unexpected and fortuitous meeting, an opportunity presented itself which showed me there was a path forward, and so here we are today with the eleventh issue of Storyteller, one I can confidently say is our best. Also, it is the first of many more to follow. The *way* is clear to me once again. There may be some changes to come, but I promise the core of what Storyteller does, its mission and purpose, has not and will not be changed. We are here for those aspiring to tell the stories in their heart, and for those wanting to know those stories.

I couldn't be more excited for this next phase of the journey, and I can't wait to introduce you to the people joining me on the Storyteller Team. Please follow us on social media (see first page) and check our website for updates and information in the days and weeks to come.

Sincerely,

Shay Shivecharan

WELCOME TO SUMMERSDALE

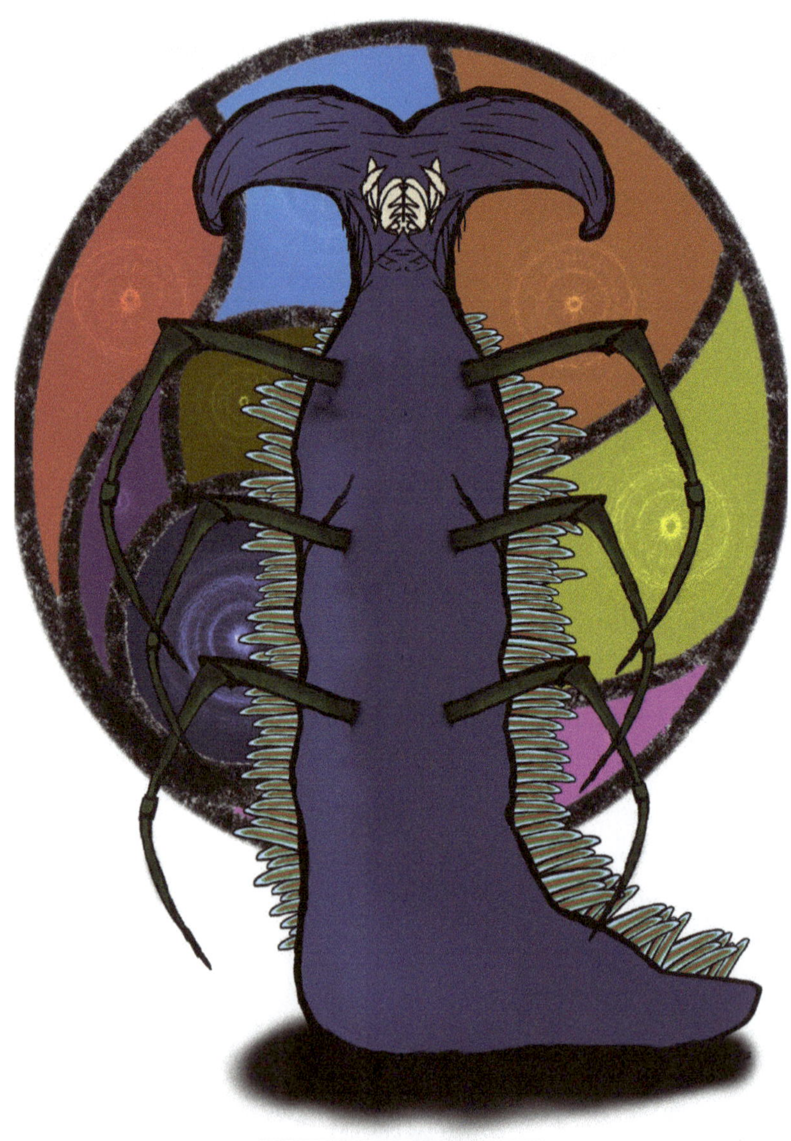

BY AARON MORRISON

"I still don't get why we are bothering with this place."

Evan tugged at the front of his t-shirt that clung to his chest. His jaw flexed as he chewed down at nothing. His tongue ran over his dry lips. His knee bounced as he looked out the window of the car. The repetitive scenery only served to annoy him further.

"I've already explained this to you, little brother."

Jackson sat comfortably in the front passenger seat. He was leaning back, legs wide, with his arm resting on the door through the open window. A backpack sat on the floor between his feet.

"Well fucking explain it again," Evan spat. "It makes zero fucking sense to stop in some retirement community when we are trying to get over the border."

"Why are you so anxious to get to the border there, killer?" Jackson smirked and laughed at his own joke. Tyson, who was driving the car, and Alicia, who sat behind Jackson, both joined in the laughter.

"Fuck you," Evan responded.

"You just need some tension released," Jackson continued. "Why don't you help him out, Alicia?"

Alicia smirked and reached over to place her hand on Evan's inner thigh, slowly moving it up.

"Don't touch me," Evan said firmly. He grabbed Alicia's wrist and shoved her arm away. Jackson and Alicia laughed.

"Like I said before, this community is loaded," Jackson explained. "The retirees built and paid for this private little town. And it's *at least* two days away from any proper emergency services. Perfect place to refuel and let off some steam."

"What makes you think they're loaded?" Evan questioned.

"What part of they built and paid for a private town did you not fucking understand?"

"That doesn't mean they have tons of cash laying around," Evan retorted.

"They're old," Jackson responded. "Old people don't trust banks. If it ain't bills, then it's jewelry. Coins. Something! Adding to the money we got on that last job, it's icing on the cake." He tapped the bag with his foot. "Even if we come up dry, it's worth taking a break from this drive. My ass is starting to chafe."

Evan's nostrils flared in disgust and he turned his head back toward the window. He watched the car behind them in the side view mirror. Both of its passengers, Barrett and Julian, had their arms dangling out of the rolled down windows. Evan could see the brown bottles in their hands. Julian, the driver, gave a flick of his wrist and the bottle shattered on the potholed and graying asphalt.

"Fucking animals," Evan muttered to himself.

A very long hour later, the sign announcing Summersdale appeared on the right, with the town itself not far beyond. Tyson took the turn a bit too fast onto the road. The car fishtailed, but he recovered quickly. Meanwhile Julian almost spun the other car out and had to stop briefly to turn and follow properly.

"Slow the fuck down," Evan admonished Tyson.

"My bad," Tyson raised a hand in acknowledgment.

"Welcome to Summersdale," Jackson said.

The town came into full view.

As they approached, Evan could see that Summersdale was spread out like a trapezoid. At the smaller base was the entrance to town, with the homes all built out towards the back.

"Pull in there," Jackson directed Tyson to a two pump gas station. Tyson pulled the car up to the far pump. Julian stopped behind them. "You and Julian fill up, then come find us," he instructed. "We'll locate the bar."

"Right," Tyson nodded.

Evan got out of the car and stretched. As he waited for Jackson to tell the others the plan, he watched a snail make its way along the side of a planter box sitting between the gas station and the road. The snail tirelessly stayed its course. The muscular waves of the foot pushed it along, leaving behind a trail of glistening mucus.

"Let's go," Jackson shoved the bag at Evan. He slung it over his shoulder. Jackson, Alicia hanging on his right arm, ordered the rest of the crew forward. The four walked down the road and into town.

Main Street was lined with the basics. A grocer. A barber. A drugstore. Everything Evan expected to see on Main Street of a small town. A few cars were parked along the road, including a powder blue classic Buick, which Evan almost bumped into.

"Nice," Evan whispered to himself as he pursed his lips in admiration.

Watchful eyes from wrinkled faces followed the group as they walked down Main Street. Small pockets of old men with slicked back hair and old women with high hairdos milled about the town or sat outside the various establishments.

"Oldtimer!" Jackson shouted at one of the men seated outside the drugstore. "Where's the bar?"

> **❝ Small pockets of old men with slicked back hair and old women with high hairdos milled about the town or sat outside the various establishments.**

The man looked the group over, then pointed further down the road and to the left side.

"Can't miss it," the man said flatly.

"Thanks, grandpa!" Alcia blew a kiss at the man and laughed.

Jackson and Alicia walked on. Evan gave a quick nod in thanks and quickly moved on. Barrett lingered back for a moment to pick out a pair of sunglasses to steal from a rotating display stand outside a shop.

Not too much further up the road, they found the bar and entered. Evan sighed in relief, happy to be in slightly cooler air. The scent of beer, cigarettes, and glass sanitizer mingled together in his nostrils.

Evan quickly scanned the bar. The bartender, an older man who looked like he had played sports in his youth, watched the four newcomers. Six high back bar stools lined the wooden bar. Two were taken by older men at the far end.

Across from the two men, a television attached high on the wall was broadcasting the bottom of the first of an Astros game. A mournful country song spilled its melancholy from the jukebox in the back right corner.

Along the back wall, the door to the "Ladies and Gents" stood cracked open. To the left of the restroom door were a set of closed double doors with "Employees Only" inscribed on the mounted signs. Four men played cards at a table in the far left corner.

"Four beers," Jackson barked.

The bartender calmly retrieved the white towel that dangled from his back pocket. He wiped his hands on the towel and returned it to its home. His expression remained unchanged, and he did not break eye contact with Jackson.

Jackson laughed and looked around incredulously.

"Are you fucking deaf?" Jackson asked aggressively.

"Just waiting for you to tell me which brand." The bartender calmly reached back and tapped the clear glass door of the refrigerator.

"Surprise me." Jackson waved his hands out sarcastically. "The balls on this guy." He grabbed Alcia by the waist and pulled her to him.

The bartender opened the fridge and pulled out four beers. The door shut with a *thwump* and the hiss of opening bottles soon followed. The falling bottle caps tinkled as they hit the bar. Evan looked away.

The four old men at the back were watching the proceedings through the thin wisps of smoke that curled up from one of the men's cigarettes.

"Evan!"

Evan looked back over at Jackson.

"Come drink your beer, fucker."

"Right." Evan clenched his jaw and walked over. He took off the backpack and wedged it securely in the gap between the brass footrest and the bar. He took a seat and picked up the bottle, raised it in a mocking toast to the others, and drank half of it in one go. Evan glanced back at the men in the corner, made brief eye contact with the bartender, and then looked down at the bar. He finished the rest of the beer.

"Another round," Jackson ordered. "Plus shots of Jack."

The bartender shrugged, and began filling the request.

"As soon as Tyson and Julian are done, we should go," Evan said to Jackson.

"We just got here, little brother," Jackson replied. "And I don't particularly like all this questioning of my plans. We do what we said we would do, and then we leave. Not before. Got it?"

Evan shifted his shoulders uncomfortably.

"Fine." Evan slammed the shot as soon as it was in front of him and chased it down with the second beer.

The sound of engines from outside the bar reached Evan's ears and then stopped. He heard two doors slam.

"About time, you dumb fucks," Barrett greeted Tyson and Julian as they walked in.

"You want to drive, shithead?" Tyson retorted.

"Fuck no."

"Then shut the fuck up."

While Tyson and Barrett argued, Julian made the two men at the end of the bar move so he could sit. One of the men moved to a table near the card players. The other exited the establishment.

Another round.

The gang, save Evan, grew louder. The crash of glass echoed up from Barrett and Julian throwing their bottles on the bar floor.

More drinks.

"Holy shit."

Tyson, who had been leaning up against the bar next to Evan, reacted to something he saw outside the open door of the bar. He strode out quickly, bottle still in hand, and grabbed the old lady that was passing by. The old lady struggled as he pulled her into the bar.

"Get a load of this." Tyson forcibly removed the bracelet the woman was wearing and tossed it to Jackson.

"Fucking told you," Jackson grinned. He handed the bracelet to Alcia. Evan glanced at the piece of gold jewelry with its inset pearl and diamonds. Barrett walked over to take a closer look. He tried to grab it. Alicia told him to fuck off and put it on her own wrist.

"You got more treasure like that, grandma?" Barrett turned to the old lady.

She nodded.

"I do."

"Woo!" Barrett shouted and clapped his hands together in one loud smack. As he turned back to Jackson, the town's sheriff walked in. He was an older man. Balding, with a wide gray mustache gracing his upper lip. His round face emanated a calm and friendly demeanor.

"Afternoon." The sheriff looked over the gang and then to the bartender. "Gus," the sheriff nodded in greeting.

"Sherriff," Gus responded.

"Well," the sheriff turned his attention back to the gang with a heavy exhale. "We don't mind visitors in our little town, but it seems you all have been causing a bit more of a ruckus than we would like. So, I would ask you kindly to finish your drinks, and move on to where you're going."

"Is that so, sheriff?" Jackson asked with a sneer.

"Jesus Christ!" Evan exclaimed too late to matter.

Tyson brought his beer bottle down on the sheriff's head while Barrett put his gun against the poor man's temple and pulled the trigger.

Blood and brain splattered out onto the bar floor.

The sheriff's body fell hard to the ground.

"What the fuck?" Evan turned to Jackson.

"You should be happy, killer," Jackson gave a nasty grin. "Now you aren't the only one with blood on his hands."

Jackson pushed himself up and away from the bar.

"If anyone even thinks about interfering with us, you'll get the same or worse," He shouted at everyone in the bar. "Now." He approached the old woman and pulled out his own gun. "You're going to show my friends here the rest of your valuables and point them in the direction of whoever else has got some nice trinkets. If you don't, well..." He put the gun near her head. "Pow. Understand?"

The woman nodded.

"Good."

Jackson motioned for Tyson, Barrett, and Julian to take the woman and escort her outside where she could lead them to the homes.

"You two!" Jackson waved his gun at two of the men. "Pick up the body, and sit him in a chair. Don't want you to forget what will happen. Now!" Jackson ended with a shout when the two men didn't immediately comply. They picked up the sheriff, sat him in a chair, and returned to their seats.

"Another round!" Jackson yelled at Gus and returned to his spot at the bar.

Alicia, still laughing at the preceding events, grabbed at Jackson's crotch.

"Makes me so hot," she licked into Jackson's ear.

Evan barely heard what was going on around him. Voices were muffled behind the ringing in his ears and everything was out of focus.

...high and inside...

...the cattle are prowlin', the coyotes are howlin'...

Jackson and Alcia began to make out.

"Think these old men like to watch," Alcia said and nodded towards the card players who hadn't stopped looking over at the bar.

"Why don't you give them a little show then?" Jackson looked back at the men.

Alicia smiled and kissed Jackson again. Their tongues intertwined like two slugs mating. A string of spit hung between the fleshy slabs as they ended their kiss.

Alicia walked over to the men, exaggerating the movement of her hips. She leaned forward, pressing her breasts together, and took the cigarette out of the smoking man's mouth. Alcia took a drag and blew the smoke into the man's face. She wiggled her ass in Jackson's direction.

The smoking man leaned back and turned his head slightly. He was clearly uncomfortable, but did not overreact.

Evan's leg bounced faster. He stretched his neck from side to side as his grip tightened around the bottle of beer.

...six-four-three double play...

...hahahaha...

...ooh-ooh-ooh-doo-di-di singin' his cattle call...

The sheriff sat with his blown out skull not even thirty feet from where Alicia was tormenting the other man.

"Enough," Evan whispered. "Enough!" he shouted and stood to grab Jackson by the front of his jacket.

"What the fuck is your problem?" Jackson shouted back. He slid his arms up between Evan's and pushed him off.

"We came to rob these people, not torture them!" Evan gestured towards the sheriff's body and Alicia.

"Fine!" Jackson threw up his hands. He acquiesced, though in a most angry and sarcastic manner. "Come back, babe. Don't want the old men to have heart attacks from the change in blood flow." He looked back at Evan. "Happy?"

Evan waved his hand and sat back down at the bar.

"When the fuck did you grow a conscience anyway?" Jackson muttered.

Alicia returned to Jackson and shook her head at Evan as she looped her arms around Jackson's shoulders.

"It's Gus, right?" Evan addressed the bartender.

"That's right," Gus nodded.

"Can I get a towel?" Evan asked.

Gus grabbed one from under the counter and handed it to Evan.

Towel in hand, Evan pushed away from the bar and walked over the sheriff's body. He placed the towel over the sheriff's face. The blood had not yet dried and soaked quickly into the fibers of the towel.

"Sorry," Evan whispered. He returned to the bar.

Jackson and Alicia scoffed and rolled their eyes at Evan before turning their attention back on eachother. Evan kept his eyes forward and ignored them while Gus poured him a shot and gave a subtle nod. Evan returned the nod and picked up the glass. After the briefest of thoughtful hesitation, he quaffed the whiskey.

The song on the jukebox changed.

Another shot.

Another beer.

...it's the top of the fifth...

"It's been way too long," Evan observed.

"What?" Jackson asked, annoyed.

"Tyson and them," Evan continued. "They should've been back by now,"

"Maybe there's a lot of loot," Jackson was dismissive.

"Or they're fucking passed out somewhere," Evan retorted.

"Fine! You want to go look for them? Be my guest." Jackson waved Evan away. Evan stood and turned toward the door. "And don't go thinking of taking the money and running out on us, little brother!"

"They have the keys," Evan responded then added "fucking idiot" under his breath as he walked out the door.

The streets of Summersdale were empty. A stillness had settled across the town and permeated the air. Evan, hands in pockets and shoulders hunched, only heard the sound of his own breathing and footsteps as he shuffled toward the homes at the back of town.

The houses were pristine and the yards immaculately kept. The largest homes were at the center, with the sizes decreasing the further out they went. The largest houses each had the same circular window in the middle of what Evan thought must be the top floor or attic. Each window had the same design, outlined in iron with three offset concentric circles. They gave the impression of a setting sun.

The front door of the house to Evan's right was open. He walked up to the house and looked around before he stepped inside.

A beer bottle on the floor gave evidence that the others had been here.

"Tyson?" Evan called out as he began to make his way into the house. "Barrett? Julian? It's time to go."

There was no response.

"Where the fuck are you?" Evan shouted even louder.

An odd, muffled sound came from around the corner to the right. Evan turned the corner and found an open door with stairs leading downward. As quietly as he could, he made his way down.

The strange sounds grew louder the farther down he went. He reached the bottom of the stairs and turned to his left.

He stumbled back and bumped into the wall.

There, in the room before him, was Barrett's naked body.

Behind Barrett's body was a creature from beyond Evan's nightmares.

Like some mix of a gastropod and insect, the creature's body arched up like a triumphant slug. Its flesh was the darkest of blues and glistened with whatever mucus it secreted. Six sectional appendages, not unlike a crab's legs, extended from its body. The ends of these extremities were buried under Barrett's skin. Two in his thighs, two in his stomach, and two in his chest.

The creature held Barrett's head with its extended maxillipeds. A proboscis from its curved, mallet shaped head had penetrated the back of Barrett's skull. Short green and orange tentacles outlined in iridescent blue covered the creature's back. Each waving independently.

Barrett twitched and his eyes moved about. A gurgling moan escaped his throat. His gaze seemed to settle on Evan.

Evan turned and bolted up the stairs. He tripped, banged his shin, and exclaimed a pained *fuck!* before he made it the rest of the way up the stairs.

Once outside again, he paused for a moment to spit out the mix of bile and whiskey that had shot up from his stomach. He spat as much of the vile taste from his mouth, then sprinted as fast as he could back to the bar.

Evan slowed to a jog and stepped back inside.

On the far end, through the now open "Employees Only" doors, Evan could see a small gathering of citizens of Summersdale.

A few other men and women had joined those that had already been at the bar. Their bodies had distended and distorted, only partially changed from their human guise to their true form. They spat out a yellowish, translucent slime that they used to cocoon Jackson and Alicia's naked bodies to the walls of the storage room.

Gus, watching from behind the bar, slightly turned his head toward Evan.

"I took enough to cover the tab," Gus said as he pointed to the bag that was now on the bar's counter. "The rest is all yours."

Gus removed a key from his pocket and held it up for Evan to see. A light *clunk* followed by a sliding noise reached Evan's ears as Gus set the key down and pushed it next to the bag. "Take it. And don't come back."

"Yeah. No problem," Evan responded.

Evan hustled to the bar to retrieve the bag and the key. He took one last glance at the scene beyond the doors, then hurried outside.

As he walked away from the bar, Evan looked down at the key and saw the three shield logo of the Buick. He clasped his hand around the key and rushed to the car.

He unlocked the door, tossed the bag into the passenger seat, and slid into the driver's seat. His left hand gripped the steering wheel while his right slid the key into the ignition.

He hesitated.

With a deep breath he turned to the bag and opened it. The remainder
of the money was there, just as Gus had said.

He turned the key, and the sweet rumble of the engine met his ears.

*...well, I figure I'll walk to the liquor store. Thunderbird, two bottles,
maybe three, maybe four...*

With a relieved smirk of a smile, Evan drove off, leaving Summersdale
far behind.

MEDIOCRITY

by Lily Perez

The bar was the place he went on the weekends

Drinking with his old college buddies, watching the game, and talking about obscene matters. Tonight was different however, as it was a Thursday, and he was already 4 beers in at 6:57 at night. His friends weren't with him even though he told his wife they'd be, and he was sitting in the corner instead of his usual stool aimed at the flatscreen. Tracing his empty glass, he looks up for the first time since he sat down in his atypical stool and notices the bartender making up another drink for the only other customer at the bar.

"Another beer Cal?" The bartender asks at the other end of the counter, Cal nods and is presented with another.

Cal kept going over the day's previous events, his boss had made an announcement that the firm had not been doing as well as last quarter so there was a chance that people were going to be let go by tomorrow. As head of employment, if there is no one to hire, then that would put Cal out of a job as well. Cal was terrified, this was what he had done for the past 12 years, he had a wife and two daughters as well as a cushy home, how could he lose all of it by Friday?

Finishing his fifth beer of the hour, he stumbles out of his stool to make his way home. The bartender notices Cal's lack of sobriety and calls out, "Let me call your wife Cal, you're in no state to be driving."

"I–Immm fine. You don't nnneed to call my wife; she doesn't nnneed– know I had one t-to mmmany on a Thursday night." Cal trips on his words.

"Let me at least call you a taxi, you can pick your car up tomorrow."

"I sss-uppose you could do that."

Cal, stumbling, gets in the taxi, and continues to contemplate, what would his wife think if he lost his job? Cal thought, "She has always been an easy woman to get along with. I don't think she'll be disappointed in me, but she loves our house and the town we live in. What if we have to move so I can look for more work? She will be devastated, as well as the girls, they love their friends."

"Make sure he gets home safe." the bartender says to the taxi driver. The taxi driver nods to the bartender and starts to drive, "Where ya headed?" Cal still drunk, and internalizing, wonders and asks, "W-What time is it?"

"Half past seven. Why? Are you late to be somewhere son?"

At this point, Cal was restless and did not want to be in that stuffy car anymore and he certainly did not want to go home drunk. He didn't want to explain to his wife yet why he had been drinking and why he had lied.

"Ssss-top the car I-I want to get out." Cal stated anxiously.

"Are you sure?" the taxi driver asks questionably.

"Yesss, l-let me out here I kn-kn-know where I-Immm going." The taxi driver brings the car to a stop and motions to the door. Cal tosses the money for the cab up to the front and stumbles out of the car. He looks left to a dark unmanaged park that no one seems to ever visit but sneaky teens and addicts. He looks right, to a long, down sloped well-lit street with a few people still moving about. Both ways would get him home but going right would take longer.

Unbalanced and stumbling he made his way down the street, thinking about his life. He thought about his childhood; he lived not far from where his current house is now, a lovely two-story yellow house in suburbia with white shutters and a white picket fence. His father, an easy well-mannered man, worked for the same firm as he does now, and his mom, a blonde with her smarts left to be found, stayed home taking care of him and his two brothers. They always celebrated birthdays with a big party (but it was just an excuse for the parents to drink) and Thanksgiving and Christmas were always at his grandparents' house who lived down the street. Every winter break they vacationed to the same Colorado ski resort without fail. He loved when his mom made him spaghetti and meatballs, and he was prom king senior year. Cal lived the typical college experience, met his wife, and got married straight out of college. He considered his best accomplishment to be predicting who won the 2016 Super Bowl. The Broncos. He was content. This was Cal's life.

Suddenly, he drunkenly stops and says loud enough people could hear down the street. "I am boring!" In that moment, Cal realized he was just like everyone else. He was boring. He had never done anything outside of the box in his entire life. None of his experiences were unique in any way. This profound epitome shocked him; he didn't know what to do after discovering this. Still drunk, all he could do was sit down in the middle of the sidewalk. Mumbling to himself, "I am an ordinary, unremarkable, stereotyped man. I am small and I am nothing." This made Cal start weeping, as he could not handle all this new original thought and self-awareness. After several minutes of crying, he heard the church clock tower chiming. "Nine o'clock." He said. He inhaled a deep sniffly breath and wiped away his tears.

Cal picked himself up and continued to wander. But he started getting angry. He was angry about the fact that he couldn't have controlled how his life went, especially if he wasn't even awake to the fact of how boring it was until now. "It's like someone wrote my story for me and I didn't even get a chance to make my own decisions!" Cal exclaims.

> **" At this point Cal was outraged, he had found the culprit of his recent discovery and all he wanted to do was attack me, whatever me was. The voice copied.**

At this point, me, the writer, is uneasy because he just figured it out. Yes, I am in control of Cal's fate. I could do anything at this point, I could even erase him becoming self-aware with himself. But I am curious to see where this goes.

"Dammit." Someone says.

Cal hears this, looks around, and asks, "Hello? Who is there?"

"Oh, crap…. You can hear me?"

"Who is this?!" Cal continues to look around and wonders if he just drank too much.

The voice copies, "Cal continues to look around and wonder if he just drank too much."

Cal, sobering, "I know I drank too much don't remind me! Who is this?!"

"Uh... your ghost?

"What?"

"Nah, I'm just kidding, you got me, I'm your narrator, or whatever you want to call me."

"Jesus, I have drank too much." Cal facepalms his forehead and lets out an annoyed groan. The voice copies again.

"God that is annoying isn't it." I state.

"Yes, quite, why don't you make it stop."

Oh *yes* let's see here... let me just press a button and *all* my narrations will stop broadcasting... WRONG. I am just as confused as you buddy."

"Well, whether this is real or not I'd like to ask you a few questions, *narrator.*"

"Go ahead, I'd like to see where this goes."

Even though I knew what Cal was going to say I still wanted to let him think he was asking an original question. The voice copies again.

"Fine! If you know what I'm going to ask, then just answer the question."

Cal wanted to know many things, like why he could hear me right now or if this was a dream or not. But on the top of his list was who wrote his story, and why did they write it so boring. The voice copied again.

"Well, if you really must know, it was me, I wrote your story."

At this point Cal was outraged, he had found the culprit of his recent discovery and all he wanted to do was attack me, whatever me was. The voice copied. Cal tried his best to ignore the fact that the writer knew his every move. The voice copied again.

"And WHY did you write it *so* boring?" Cal questioned angrily.

"Well, honestly, because I wanted a good writing challenge, and this seemed like a good subject to jump off from."

"Well, did you even take into consideration my life? My feelings?"

"No, I hadn't actually, because I did not expect for you to hear me writing your story!"

"Well, what is going to happen tomorrow as I go into work and find out if I get to keep my job or not?"

"I can't disclose that information that would ruin the ending."

"Why the hell not?!"

"I just told you, besides I haven't quite yet decided what your fate is."

At this point, we had been bickering all night and the sun was starting to come up. Cal was in his clothes from the day before, so he was ready to go back into work even though he had been up all night. The voice copied again.

"You know, you had a good life before you realized this, yeah it was textbook stereotype, but you were happy and content. What's so wrong about that?"

"I suppose you're right. I just hate that I had to realize it all tonight."

"Yeah, sorry."

As Cal fixed his clothes to head to work, he stopped at the coffee place he went to each morning as it was close to work, and got a black coffee, two creams, two sugars just like he did every morning. The voice responded.

"Hey! Stop that. Black coffee, really? Could you have written me any more boring?" Cal said in annoyance.

"Nope, can't get more boring than this." Me, the narrator states.

Cal looks to the sky in annoyance once more, since that's the only place he hears me, and continues his walk to work. Once he gets to his building, he stops for a moment to prepare for whatever news he is going to hear. As he continues through the glass doors of the firm, he greets the front desk ladies with a hung-over smile, sleepy eyes, and vaguely disheveled attire. He enters the elevators to the right of the front desk and clicks floor 10. As he ascends, he gets more and more nervous about his fate. The doors open and he makes his way to his desk, greeting his coworkers along the way. Everyone looks just as nervous as him when his boss makes his way out of his office to make the big announcement.

"Alright everybody, sorry to keep you waiting, I was up for the better half of the night with the people upstairs to figure out what the final decision is. With great pleasure, I would like to announce that we found money in the budget to keep all of you!"

Cheers and claps light up the room and Cal's face goes from exhausted and anxious to excited and celebratory. "I am truly sorry if I put unnecessary stress on all of you and I'm sure the wives weren't too pleased either." Boss man says with an apologetic tone. "All in all, have a good and productive workday folks, I'm sure you'll all be celebrating tonight." At this point, Cal realized he got all worked up for nothing, everything could go back to normal if he wanted. He subconsciously agreed with his writer that he was content and happy before realizing his life was boring. The voice copies.

"I'm ready." Cal says in a content manner.

Cal went about his day and had dinner with his family in the evening like he did every night, he was happy, and he was content. Thinking the night before was just a dream due to his overuse of alcohol.

THE IN-BETWEEN OF LOVE
BY LISA BUI

To her, love was just another business

Another negotiation. Her work ethic was so deeply ingrained in her personality that it conditioned her every decision. She sought only to yield the best outcome. Romance was inevitably taken out of the equation, removing the equality of the functions of two lovers and replacing it with "less than" or "greater than".

She must have forgotten about the love she taught me.

The night before my mother left my father and the family they built together, I laid motionless on my bed, trying to shrink my existence as much as possible under the crumpled white blanket. My tears soaked into the soft fabric. The sleepless night cast a delusive atmosphere through our three-room apartment – his, hers, and mine – like how the sea pretended to be calm before a storm struck like a juggernaut. After more than three decades of "us against the world," she had decided to end their companionship.

I sniffed the blanket's lavender scent, hoping to soothe my racing thoughts. Out in the living room the TV played classic Christmas tracks, but all I could pick up was their yelling. He cried. She cried. Me? I lay in bed, trying to absorb every detail, every word, even though it made my heart drop. Like a bat out of hell, my focus gravitated to all the undesirable emotions.

I woke up to a harsh silence, contrasting the shouts and sobs from earlier. I must have fallen asleep, emotionally exhausted after listening to the muffled crying. I got up from bed and walked over to my mother's bedroom, full of dread. I knocked on her door, holding back the force. I half-heartedly asked, "Mom, are you okay?"

Silence.

Then, a sob, followed by the shattering of a glass bottle, presumably one of the cheap beers she bought at the 7/11.

"If you need to talk, I'm here, Mom," I pressed on.

I wanted no more of this drama. I was exhausted from the endless nights, being kept awake by their shouting. I was tired of being overlooked when I tried to help, only to be dismissed. My patience was wearing thinner and thinner everytime I knocked and there was no answer.

I tried to check up on my dad instead, but he was nowhere to be found. What ugly wreckage this home had become.

Boxes were packed and piled up, ready to be taken out of the house she was so desperate to leave. I didn't believe she genuinely wanted to. She just had to win.

What is love, anyway? The lessons, the stories, and the experiences I witnessed growing up were no longer relevant. The example that was supposed to be so strong and solid that it made me want to follow it and find love of my own had broken apart.

Tuesday came. Still curled up under my blanket, all I heard was the rapid footsteps towards the front door and the rhythmic rollings of the wheels on her suitcase. I heard boxes dragged across the floors, followed by her exit. A sharp snap of the door. Noises. That's what I could remember. I knew she was leaving but couldn't pull myself together enough to get out of bed and run to her, to beg her one final time to stay, even if I knew it wouldn't work.

In the months that followed, I tried as hard as I could not to recall the day she left. I wondered, if only I'd opened the door that night, would I have found her curled around herself? Crying like my father would the following New Year's Eve? I would find him curled up in a fetal position as if he was trying to seek security in his mother's womb, crying in agony, unable to salvage his own family. My mother had always been recognized for her success. For the altruistic sacrifices, she made for her child and husband, and for her philanthropic heart. She was so used to the spotlight, but my father was never given credit for his own unspoken sacrifices. The more she bathed in that glory, the worse my father was patronized. If it wasn't her way, it must be the wrong way. If he couldn't even love the right way, what would be left of him?

. . .

She had been lost, curled up in her own illusions of love. What is love, anyway? A gruesome fantasy of possession and authority, manipulation and guilt, and, of course, the deception of altruism. Oh, she was well aware of all these undesirable realities, but God knew she barely made an attempt to break free, trapping her damned soul in a senseless consciousness.

She was free, or so she thought. She was whole again, or was that just a figment of a predetermined performance, designed by whoever was pulling the strings in her head? Her emotions and thoughts were just a series of codes coordinated by whoever was programming the course of her actions, conditioning her to be the way she was. Unapologetically unfiltered. It was a repetitive awakening and falling back into that surrealistic rabbit hole. The only way was through. But every time she tried to push through, those unresolved feelings snooping behind her resentment and guilt locked around her ankle and wouldn't let her move forward. They denied her an opportunity for redemption, chaining her to her biggest foe: herself.

She just wanted to be loved. She just wanted to be forgiven. She just wanted to be released from the relentless tension and the back and forth of unnecessary fights. But could one become liberated if she was never oppressed? She was obsessed with the attention and refused to accept its absence.

. . .

"She is gone. I am worthless. No more fights. But I miss her."

"Dad, you need time to heal. Just give her time, too."

"You don't get it. How helpless and useless I feel ..."

His nights are restless and his mornings have turned into nightmares. She's not there when he wakes up, so why should he even bother sleeping? The anxiety and guilt drill into his conscience, drowning him in relentless battles of blame and shame. How many days has it been? He doesn't even remember.

Peace. Shock. Shaking. Tears.

"Dad, what are you doing on the floor?" I ask him as he curls up on the floor with his arms around his knees, squeezing so tight the veins in his arms look like they might burst from the effort of holding himself together. I can tell he hasn't taken a shower in days. His hair is uncombed and oily. His face is red and blotchy, tears trailing down his cheeks from tight-shut eyes, squeezing as if it were the only way to expunge all the pain. At first, it's like a noir silent movie until, finally, he can't hold it any longer. His voice cracks when he tries to speak.

"...."

"It's okay, it's gonna be okay. I'm here..." I whisper as I gather myself around him, trying to brush through his oily hair with my fingers to soothe his discomfort.

"...."

"I'm so sorry, dad."

"I love your mom so much, but now she's gone. I'm not enough. I didn't do enough," he says in a trembling voice. Then, all of a sudden, he starts to sob. The sobbing turns into a boiling cry and sputtering of meaningless words. A cry of anger.

FRANGIPAIN
by Gabrielle Roessler

There are a lot of things I didn't write about

I'm not sure if it was because the words never looked right, if it was too painful, or if somehow seeing it spilled out on a clean blank page made reality too sharp at the edges. But I remember it was vividly, undeniably OVER when I hurled the plumeria cutting into the dumpster. His mother had given it to me as a blessing but, in retrospect, I see it as a clumsy preemptive olive branch. The sap was thick, sticky, and matte porcelain. She warned me not to get it on my car or it would eat through my paint. I got it all over my fingers, my thighs, and the back patio where it pooled and reminded me daily for three weeks that suffering is a lengthy process that is easy for others to look away from.

I didn't cry like I thought I would when I snapped it in half, the edges sharp and bleeding milk between rusted shears. I also didn't cry when it echoed in the trash bin almost a month later, an offering of boxed thunder – the first in a long list of banishing spell ingredients from my therapist. Definitely not when I thought about it rotting in the stench and heat beneath a blistering summer orange, low in the sky.

But I did cry every time I showered. And on first dates where I knew from the moment we said "hello" there would be no seconds.

There are still a lot of things I don't write about. Bringing them up feels like undoing all the sweat and labor that went into creating that grave, unnecessarily tilling earth that was finally ready for greener things. Trauma is the touch of gunmetal gray on the passenger side of my black Chevy, something I don't think about until I remember I'm not in Jersey and have to pump my own gas. Until someone rubs their fingernail in the gritty groove with a crinkled nose and says I should fix it because everyone else can see it.

But the man who rides shotgun now – legs too long, crowded happily next to the dash for the last three years – takes it in stride. He sees my exposed foundations and praises the surrounding polish that still holds its own. When the smell from the emotional body bags in the backseat gets too cloying, he rolls down the windows and points out Toy Story clouds and fluffy brown cows.

These are the things I write about because they are the propagations I celebrate. These are the cuttings I saved and cultivated into something greater than the sum of their parts.

The Doomsday Parade: A Collection

by Blake Slaughter

Thanksgiving

Here I am: Irreconcilably wrecked with emotion. It physically tears at me as I sit in this folding chair low as my ambitions. It was Thanksgiving, but I had nothing to give this year. My only possession was a fight for life, my own life, that is. At times these words give ease, at others, a maddening reminder of my immovable nature.

The pain is a hunger insatiably feasting at my insides, with its fangs and fate-ridden scenarios. I threw away the bottles, flushed the pills, and did just about all but relinquish my will. It's always inadequate. Will it ever not be? If another has the answer, why, oh, why won't you share it with me?

A Tombstone for Timothy Stranger

From fields of green I plot your demise. Seas will flow, oceans dare rise. My hand paints the horizon with red, derived from you. Leave me for dead. Turn me on, let me loose. The rising moon greets with lunar curiosity, and I am left speechless: a revenant, an oddity.

Do you dare gaze beyond the oil canvas; where I stand unabashed, unbruised, unrepentant? Kill me swiftly with closed eyes tight. Cut me open baby. Bleed me dry. The body you touched is only a conduit— for I've seen the end; in disaster, I'm fluent. Raise the blade a second time. I stab back. I draw the line.

Mark my grave in this unlit foyer and tell them I've gone missing: my friends and employers. Where is one to go when life is devoid? Will I end it all or become another gone boy?

Unnamed

To the girls who didn't make it out alive— those people who gave up the ghost. I raise to you, a half-full glass in toast. I wish I could have protected you; could have wiped the tears: 'For you were gone too soon. This puzzle, this labyrinth, this Godforsaken ire, it unraveled in abundance, so you set yourself on fire. Did you do it for love, for the pain, for the end? From the other side of the grave, I reach out. Touch my hand.

Pacifists and activists at war within themselves, while the here and the now sit upon some distant shelf. Maybe I'm cured or possibly distracted, though this illness of ours could never be extracted. I think of you all in the coffee shops and grocery marts. Perhaps I've mastered the art of falling apart.

Warning Clouds

I have done it again, my God. It seems I excel in these matters of dependency and mimicry, as I am only that of those around me unless I am spiraling— in which I am the master. Yes, the speck of dust has not gone unnoticed; that is a talent all of my own. No, these four walls on the west side could never bring comfort, nor never be home. I cannot maintain function without a secondary heart to pump alongside mine. I cannot surrender these lonely feelings— My God, have I done it this time!

I look to the Nebraskan planes for answers but find none. They only offer short deliverance from suicidal ideation. Those ideas are clouds. They are storms brewing on the flat horizon and they're coming our way. So, we best be heading inward if there is a fair amount of hell to pay.

Flatirons

I wish I had died in the Flatiron hills— fallen perchance from the rock-formed staircase into the dead and dried grass laying way to the city. I wish the boulders had caressed and caved me in— that Boulder would have offered my life for the taking.

Though, what if the Gorge had swallowed me whole and I gave it all up: body and soul? The Black Hills are dreamscapes I wake from with lust. The desolate planes— I must return, I must.

Forever I wished to be found in this world, devoid of that knowledge in its consequence. Can I muster that strength, that hunger for knowledge? Reverse it, allow the loss, follow it.

Dear Johnny Cash *by Nicholas Michael Reeves*

Dear Johnny Cash,

There's that little sliver of
Stevie Nicks in every woman,
that shade of Johnny Cash black
in every man.

The wounded gypsy,
the minor prophet of hurt,

ballading heaven,
raising hell.

Arms too short to
box with God, but
swinging for
his turned cheek
anyhow,

an act of worship,
when compared to
kissing it.

I first met you driving
down the backroads of
old Kansas,

the grain of the radio

and the flame of your voice

finding all the dark parts of me.

You turned my old truck a

church. Hymnals for the heathens.

Old family recipes from Eden.

Eighteen years, I never met

God in a pew. Not the first

edition of him, anyhow.

I needed stories, not dogma.

I needed to know that

even shame could be forgiven.

You taught my cold heart

how to weave her

wounds into worship.

That bass-baritone, pitch-black

pitch. Those songs of

salvation, damnation,

knocking on the door

of Judgement Day

with all the drugs,

all the whiskey,

and the Kingdom of God

inside you.

I drove and we sang,

you prayed and I amened

until I was at mother's grave again.

Humbled by your words.

Momma, let me tell you,

I'm sorry for what I became.

I'm the same boy you

used to kiss, I promise,

beneath this black

I shine.

I needed your words.

America did too.

A country slit at

the throat with Vietnam,

civil rights, inequality.

Music is the only thing that told the truth.

Textbooks, they lie about history, invent it.

But songs, they are history.

History of the soul.

Aren't I glad there was
Johnny, the nice one, and Cash,
who caused all the trouble.

Someone honest enough to save us,
to walk the line. To write about what hurts.

Like Shelley's Frankenstein,
you wrote, I'm made up of bad
parts but trying to do good.

You were only five years old when your
dad shot your dog for eating the hogs' scraps.

Twelve when you dug your brother's grave
with a shovel, the morning of his funeral.

And having stepped on a nail, sat barefoot
in the pews, covered in mud,
while the preacher said some words.

Who knew at fourteen, Jack could die?
There was a time I didn't believe in death either.

But as the table saw spilled his guts
across the floor, and as he crawled
to you for help, you learned quickly.

I imagine that's when Cash was born, with
that first cigarette at twelve years old.

Soon our uncle shipped you off to
Germany, where you bought your first guitar.

Then you were touring,
flushing lit cherry bombs down hotel toilets,
throwing television sets out of penthouse
windows, setting animals free in hotels.

Next you were in Mississippi,
stumbling home drunk at 2:00 a.m.,
arrested for picking dandelions.

And, not a moment too soon, June.
June got you sober.
You named her breasts
Rose and Anne.

Then you named your
first child Rosanne.

She died in May,
and of course, you followed.

The first line of the *Tennessean* read,
"Somehow, Johnny Cash is dead."

Somehow. Oh, but we know how.

How heaven, to you, was
morning, coffee, and her.

How when all the lights turned
out and everyone went home,
it was you and her.

You could lose the
stage, the words, the song,
hell, even your soul.

Because the first time you did,
June brought it back.

But flesh and
blood needs flesh
and blood.

And what was
July without June?

RIDING FUMES

BY JOSHUA MAHN

I I was shaken back to reality as my entire car rattled violently against a pothole

---

My head snapped up and, dreamy-eyed and trying to keep my wits about me, I glanced at the needle on my fuel gauge.

Hovering just over E. I figured I must've had 30 miles or so left, at best.

Though I could feel my muscles tensing in avoidant protest, I returned my attention towards the rear-view mirror.

Still behind me.

My phone sat dead in my cup holder amongst a pair of forgotten coins. Its open-casket pallor reflected only smudged fingerprints instead of the comforting light of the GPS, which called it quits ages ago.

I must have missed my turn at some point, but god only knows when that could have been. These pocked and featureless desert roads had slid by me for what felt like an eternity. I'd sat daydreaming with a marked dissociative disinterest for almost the entire time.

To be honest, I was hardly even aware of the fact that I was still driving.

I was completely certain that any obvious forks in the road would have been enough excitement that I'd have noticed them from miles out. Yet, I'd been heading in this same direction for so long. I must have missed something important. It only made sense.

Maybe I should've pulled a U-turn then and there, as soon as I had this epiphany, but instead I pressed on with a dysfunctional optimism that my way would become clear soon.

In any case, I knew I burned more gas heading in this direction than I've got left, so turning around would have been completely useless. Even in the waning dregs of daylight I had left, I could see clearly for miles and miles around me. Nothing but an ocean of hot sand broken up by the occasional jagged form of a stubborn cactus. I couldn't even see any city lights.

It probably would've been gorgeous out here, if I wasn't so damned nervous.

Anyway.

Still right behind me.

I'd been driving this way for so long by myself, at some point I'd become vaguely aware that I wasn't alone out there any longer. Though I was sleepy and full of daydreams, it struck me as odd that anything could have crept up on me in such a barren and empty environment without my noticing; slipping up behind from some unknown sideroad, or else accelerating powerfully behind me, or whatever else they did to appear.

But they were here, and they were right behind me.

I never was much of a car person, but I couldn't help but stare. It was a curious-looking thing.

The car looked old. It was long and elegant, and, even beneath the thick layer of dust which covered its surface I could see an elaborate silver filigree design etched all over its deep black paint.

It must have been terribly lavish when it was new. It still carried an air of antiqued importance. Sharp geometric designs crept across the face of its hood, forming into a shape which reminded me in an inexplicable way of some forgotten temple. This art filled me with an arcane sort of discomfort, as if I were seeing something that I wasn't fully supposed to understand.

Though one of its bulbous headlights was dim and cracked, as if laced with cataracts, its beady counterpart threw a persistent yellow glare right into my mirror with an astonishing vigor.

Try as I might, I couldn't see even a glimpse of the driver. The car's windshield was impenetrably dark, voidlike and opaque. I wondered how they were able to drive as they were. The longer I spent on the subject, the worse their headlight dazzled me.

As fascinated as I was by this traveler, I had also begun to grow antsy from their presence. They were driving a scant few feet behind my bumper; their one headlight throwing such a persistent and eerie haze into my cabin. I averted my eyes and adjusted the mirror and gripped my steering wheel tightly.

My nerves were worn thin from the drive and I was too damned sleepy for road rage. I would have rathered if they kept some distance, or passed me entirely. I must have wasted another few miles, thinking they'd change their course at some point. That they'd grow more patient, or less so, but doing something, anything differently.

When it didn't work, and my own patience wore thin, I hoped to give a bit of a hint. I tapped my brakes gently to flicker my rear lights at them. Once, twice, thrice.

In turn, they too tapped their brakes, one, twice, thrice,
 perfectly maintaining their bafflingly close proximity.

I took a breath, attempting to center inward, and resigned myself to the possibility that they'd be driving like this for as long as they saw fit, and held onto a slim hope. If they were headed this way, well then, maybe there was somewhere to go. Maybe they knew something I didn't.

My nerves remained heightened despite my best efforts. Being low on fuel and rather lost didn't make the situation any easier. The beady eye of this unwelcome and ancient follower was pushing me further and further into my own paranoia.

I lowered my drivers-side window and waved irritably as I slowed down, practically begging them to pass me.

"Go on, now! Just pass me then!"

They only slowed down behind me.

I turned my blinker on, waving harder, as if I was trying to paddle myself away from danger. My speedometer crept down, down, down. 45 miles per hour. 35. 20. I gave the brakes a firm kick.

Five miles per hour.

I crept delicately off of the road, fearful of becoming stuck in the sand but glad at the hope of removing this tailgater from my ass.

"Get it over with!" I groaned. "Go!"

I rolled at last to a dead stop.

Adjusting my mirror, I peered back towards their windshield, hoping to project some image of confidence. I hoped to see them take their chance to blast past me, leading the way to wherever it was they were headed. I hoped not to see them again.

Instead, their smooth and dry-rotted tires crunched into the sand on the side of the road, rolling to a gentle stop as I did.

My stomach felt sour. I knew then I wasn't their obstruction; I was their goal. Their destination. They were going to follow me. No matter what I did.

I clenched my steering wheel so hard that I feared I may break it, wishing I knew if I even had a tire iron to use as a weapon. I'd heard of stranded motorists doing so before. I wished to look brave and resourceful, and above all to put an end to this strange dance.

"Go away!" I shouted back at their car. My hand flitted to my door's lock, hoping to maintain one last, precious boundary. I couldn't quite grasp it, and I cursed myself for doing something wrong as the locks engaged and disengaged again and again. I forced my door's lock into a "down" position, though I could feel it vibrate in protest beneath my thumb. Despite my struggles, I thought I heard a click emanating from behind. Was it the sound of their door opening?

"Fuck it," I muttered. Knowing how irresponsible it was to use my remaining dregs of fuel in this way, slammed my gas pedal to the floor. My engine hiccuped and the fuel needle bobbed ever lower towards E, but I couldn't really think of a better plan. I couldn't really do much thinking at all.

There wasn't much of a step two, besides some hope of putting a few extra feet between us in my Hail Mary across the desert. However, even despite the many apparent years between our vehicles' manufacture, the black car kept perfect distance, rolling out of the sand and back onto the ancient asphalt with ease. I had no indication that their engine was struggling as mine was. In fact, I wasn't sure I could hear any sound at all from their car.

"Just go! Leave me alone!" I hollered out of my window, certainly red faced and spitting as I laid on my horn for emphasis. "There's a whole goddamned desert to share!"

Despite this tantrum, my adrenaline began to wane. I could feel my eyes glazing over. The monotony of this drive, interspersed with my acute agitation, was not doing me any favors.

I was too tired of this. Too tired for this. Too tired.

I clenched the steering wheel even tighter and fumbled with my phone for a few seconds, hoping it was magically restored.

It wasn't.

I cast it back into its resting place, jangling the forgotten coins, and slapped the buttons on my radio.

I was treated to nothing but static.

Too tired. My eyelids began slumping, creeping towards each other. All I had to do was keep on the gas. Keep driving until I found an exit or something. Just get to my next chance. Just get there without falling asleep.

Visions of some safe place soothed my anxious mind. There'd be a big, clean gas station with lots of friendly people nearby who could tell the other car to scram. They'd be good with directions, and things would be okay. Things would be just fine. This dream suited me quite well.

I was shaken back to reality as my entire car rattled violently against a pothole. My head snapped up and, dreamy-eyed and trying to keep my wits about me, I glanced at the needle on my fuel gauge.

Hovering just over E.

THE DIRECTION OF UP

by Gabriel McLeod

It was the bright days of summer

where the heat burned away any hopes of clouds and the sun ruled the sky, searing the land with white hot intensity, igniting the blue of the atmosphere to an opaque oblivion. It was the days before the requirement of shirts or shoes and sunglasses were rarely worn. The asphalt shimmered in the heat and blistered the soles of those who did not move fast enough. I ran everywhere in those days, blinded by the white light running down the burning streets, across scorching sidewalks, roasting parking lots into the bristling green grass, under the shade of Magnolias and Oaks, but only for a moment to catch heaving and laughing breaths, to focus gathering eyesight and easing fevered soles before running off again into the next adventure around the corner. I wasn't sure of the time, for time held little meaning then but it was before my brother was born and the 80's hovered hungrily upon the horizon.

It was days of watermelons and dragonflies, of bubblegum, boyish bravados and bicycle ramps. Days of wild plum and crab apple trees, of blue jays and blue crabs. It was the days of months away at Grandparents' houses, of weeklong trips to Gulf Shores where the powder soft dunes were as high as mountains and the turquoise waters licked your face with a million frothy tongues. It was days of slingshots and shooting stars, of dozens of open doors and dreams. It was the days before the sadness, before the shadows, before the storm. I was 6 or 7 years of age but it didn't matter, I was young and ignorant to the fact that youth or the flames of summer could ever end.

We lived on Monarch Avenue, a narrow street in the heart of the universe that led uphill to a shopping center on the right and a long road to the left that wound down through dense woods and off to the city of Mountain Brook. Behind my house was a dandelion littered green field that ended into a small park, scarred down one side by a deep run off ditch with sewer tunnels on both ends, one of which connected to a great and sparkling creek. All my friends along Monarch were girls, from the vibrant blond Thrasher sisters, Kayla and Julie and the older brunettes, Jill and Stacey, to the shy dark-haired Kris whose mother raised rabbits and to the red headed freckle speckled face of Christine Trailkill. The only other boys that were my friends lived further away: Aaron Thornton was at least 4 to 5 blocks in a wealthier neighborhood one direction and Vince Farelli was on the other side of the shopping center. Most of my time was spent with Vince who, despite bouts of occasional cruelty, was my best friend.

The humble shopping center held: a laundry mat, a grocery store, a local pub, a knick-knack shop and a barber shop where the barber, Bob Baker, knew my father well but would always call me ugly when I passed by. I made a point of avoiding the barber shop when I could. Behind the center was the meeting place for Vince and I, a delightful world of wooden crates and pallets, where the ground was hued with rainbows from oil spills and broken glass. In the back corner sat a huge dumpster we explored for thrown out groceries, fascinating odds and ends and stacks of previous month's unpurchased Penthouse and Hustler magazines. The center and back lot were circled by a patch of woods, meager in girth but towering with pines. By cutting across Monarch and through Old Lady Moody's front yard, over through her neighbor's backyard, the woods could be entered with little witness. If any vandalism or loud mischief occurred one could exit unseen, quickly and safely, the same way reversed. The back dock of the shopping center and patch of trees were our clubhouse and fort, our castles to siege, our wilderness to tame. At the far end of the center, through the trees lay an abandoned house and next to it was where Vince lived.

It was on one of those nameless, shameless days during that summer, blinded by the heat, burning feet from the street that I ran off to meet Vince. The day was ripe with plans: war games and secret missions, tree scaling and rock skipping, snacks of honeysuckle and wild blackberries. We met behind one of the houses on the outskirt of the trees and frolicked furiously in youthful abandonment. We swam in the ditch, threw mud clods at each other and against the concrete, climbed our favorite branches only to jump down and take off again, running with the speed of wind. Towards the end of the afternoon we made it back to our home base, the back of the shopping center. I had found a long green glass 7-Up bottle and gave it to Vince, which he quickly threw against the side of the wall in a glittering explosion. Within seconds the back door burst open and out came an eruption of obscenities from a booming adult voice, whose face we could not see as we dove into the safety of the trees. We hid in silence, under the overgrowth, barefoot amongst the pine. When it seemed to be evident that the glass breaking culprit had fled, the adult went back in cursing again.

It was shaded but just as warm inside there as the sunlight broke through the top branches and danced in jagged patterns along the narrow fledgling forest floor. In the deepest crux of trees in a small clearing we gathered, debating what to be done with the rest of our afternoon. The sun had way passed its zenith and began the slow climb down into dusk. When the glare softened, that was usually the time to wrap up the adventures and head home to meet parents coming home from work. We decided to scale one more tree and then look through the windows of the abandoned house next to his, trying to get home before getting into trouble for a change. This was very difficult when time held little meaning.

In the clearing we approached one exceptionally tall tree with low sprouting branches, perfect for foot holds. As I stepped, I felt my foot bow down with an almost elastic type of surface. I brushed away some part of the pine straw strewn ground and found a large piece of ply board. I tapped my foot again and felt its resistance. I then stomped against it and my foot bounced back slightly. The board had a pliant tension to it, flexible though it was against the ground. My mind quickly resolved that it was made of a magical, bouncy material. I jumped on it once, rebounding higher than a normal leap.

"Whoa!" I exclaimed, while Vince just glanced back, already working his way up the lower branch.

"Hey! This board bounces! Look!"

"You are just jumping regularly."

"No, no, for real! Look!" I stepped off the board onto the normal ground and jumped in two short bursts. Then, I stepped back on the board, feeling the place where it seemed springiest and jumped, what seemed almost twice as high as before.

"Still looks the same."

"No way!" I jumped again and again, higher each time, feeling the obvious difference between the gravity of the ground and the leaps that this magical piece of board provided.

"See! Whoa! I told you... whoa!" Higher I jumped, feeling as if I could reach the treetops above. Kangaroo like I continued, with each jump springing up into the air, grinning like a jack o lantern, laughing like a fool.

"You should stop."

"Not yet, watch. Bet I can hit those leaves!" Up I jumped, landing again, feeling the tension and bouncing higher. "Almost!" I yelled and then coming down there was a horrible cracking sound and then the trees shot out into the sky and there was an explosion of white stars as my head hit something hard, my body soaring downwards until colliding into a wet crunch and complete darkness swallowed me.

Not sure how long I was out, stunned I stirred to the sound of a voice far away.

"Hey!" It was Vince from somewhere up above.

Upside down, I was laying on my head and the top of my shoulders, my legs above and one arm was twisted behind my back. I rolled over and hit something hard but slick. I slipped around in pain. In a panic I thrust myself forward, trying to straighten my limbs against the confined strangeness. I was surrounded by slime in a small hole. Everything washed so black I couldn't see my own hand scrambling before me for reason, for direction, for explanation. Rapidly I flipped and rolled, kicking out, flailing against the dark surface that encased me, finding no edge, no exit. Not being sure which direction was what, the darkness compressed around me, closing in, crushing my breath and body. Somehow my feet found ground and pushed my legs upward. Losing the direction of up is a horrifying sensation and robs the brain of reason. Discovering which direction that was, there seemed to be more room. I concentrated on catching my breath.

I stood; feet sunken in some sort of oozing surface where a dark wall encircled me half an arms length in all directions. All was a dark pitch except straight up, where a circle of daylight was eclipsed by Vince's peering down head.

"Hey!"

"I fell down... Heh..."

"I know."

The situation had not yet sunk in completely. I was still trying to figure out how one could be jumping one moment and thrust into where I was within a second.

"Well... you should get out."

I looked around and saw nothing but the glossy dark surface all around me. The hole above seemed so far away.

"I don't think I can... can you help?"

"How?"

"I don't know... can you get me a branch or something?"

His face disappeared from the light. I could make out the trees so far up above, the space between with the color of the sky moving away from its bright white and into a dark powder blue. Vince didn't come back right away and a nervous thump began in my heart. As long as he was there, I could still have hope. My mind, still trying to understand what happened, was anxious to get out quickly.

"Hey! You up there?" I called out as the seconds ticked away.

I heard scuffling and then his shadow appeared again. Dirt and pine straw tumbled down, landing on my face. I saw a long object stretching down, some broken branch he had found and was using to reach me.

"There. It is all the way. Can you get it?"

I reached up as high as I could, feeling the ache of the fall twinge in my arm and shoulders. The branch was still way too far away. I tried to jump up a little, stretching my fingers as far as they could go but to no avail.

"I can't..."

"Here..." he reached down lower but dropped it. It broke in two against the wall, scratching my cheek.

"You dropped it."

"It fell."

"It looked like you just dropped it."

"Well, I didn't"

"Oh."

"I have to go soon. I am going to be in trouble."

"Uh... well, can you find something else? Like a vine or rope or something?"

"I told you to stop."

"I know."

He disappeared and that nervous thump started again from inside me. I looked around, still nothing but a long dark well of confusion.

"You up there?" Trying hard not to let the rising tension show in my voice. After a few minutes of no answer, I tried again, this time a little louder...

"ARE YOU THERE?"

No answer.

The wind blew and caused the branches to shiver.

"ARE...?" I started and Vince's silhouette again appeared in the circle of shine above.

"Here, try this..." He held a thin rope in his hands and lowered it over the edge. It barely reached a foot or two down, not even a portion of the depth I was at.

"It's not going to reach. It's too short."

"Well, that's all I can find."

"Look harder."

"I have to go."

"Can't you just see first?"

"I have to go. I'm supposed to be in the house when Mom gets home or I am on restrictions again."

"But I can't get out. I want to go home too."

"I told you to stop."

"I know."

And then Vince stood up, the sunlight reflecting off of his glasses, his face obscured by shade. He turned around and left. I could hear his footsteps crunching through the pine straw and out of the trees.

I called out his name. There was no response.

I waited longer this time and tried again with the same results. Only silence answered.

Part of me really thought he would go home and get his mother who would come back and help. Maybe even call the fire department again to rescue me.

One time I had been playing in the back yard and noticed a kitten had

> **" And though I called out, no one would hear me down here. I tried to yell for help a few times, hearing my own voice echo muffled off the walls of the hole. I began to tremble.**

climbed to a very high branch and got stuck. Too afraid to turn around or climb down, it sat on that branch and mewed the most pitiful and desperate cry. I felt so bad to see it so helpless and not trying to climb, or jump, too, afraid to do anything but cry out. It trembled in fear. As a great tree climber with strong hero potential, I took it upon myself to go up and rescue it.

I climbed the tree no problem, even shimmying across the branch with ease to where the frightened kitten was. As I got closer, softly trying to coax the animal into my arms, it easily jumped off and scampered off safely. When I tried to turn around, I started to slip and then clung in the same place, too afraid to move. The tree seemed taller, the branch way longer than when I began. I cried out, trembling, to my Mom until she came out. After several attempts to help, and trying to coax me down, she gave up and called the fire department. I stayed up there for what seemed like forever, clutching the bark with white knuckled desperation. Eventually they showed up with their bright red engine and ladders, climbed up and rescued me.

But this was much different. This wasn't up in a tree, I was under the ground. And though I called out, no one would hear me down here. I tried to yell for help a few times, hearing my own voice echo muffled off the walls of the hole. I began to tremble.

After a few minutes it truly sunk in. My heart started beating harder. I was trapped.

I began to look around the dark. From the dim light above I could see the grimy glaze of the circular chamber I was in. A clammy, rotten odor saturated the air. My toes squished in the substance beneath my feet. Turning I noticed a small drain pipe by my legs, a trickling sound came from within. It seemed harder to catch my breath. I took long gasps, my brain rushing to figure a way out. I could distinguish the color of my blood on my chest and fingers, feel its warmth on my cheek. My head began to throb and the hurt spread down my neck and shoulders. The pain seemed to come from all over. I cried out for help again and hearing the desperation in my own voice unleashed a flood of emotion. I started crying uncontrollably. I screamed out to Vince, to Vince's mother, to my Mom, to any one that would listen.

No one did. No one came.

Not after many long minutes, not after an hour or more. An hour to a child is an awful, intangible thing; its passing is slow and arduous, especially with nothing but anxiety to occupy your mind. I stood sobbing, staring helplessly up, waiting on someone to peer in, to hear me, to reach down with long elastic arms and save me. But there were only the movements of the trees above and the light of the sun growing darker, away from its expanding blue hue to more of a sinister and suffocating orange. I cried until all the tears were wrenched out, until the sobs slowed into long steady breaths.

It was getting dark. Vince's parents would have been home by now and they were not coming. My mom would be home too but she wouldn't know what happened or even where I was. To top it all off, if I did make it out, I would definitely be in trouble.

I leaned and pressed my forehead against the slime in defeat. I felt a tickling against my ear and jerked back to see a long millipede reaching for my hair. I swatted it aside and noticed more along the cracks of the wall, earthworms wriggling beside my feet, tiny black eyes and twitching antennae of cockroaches and crickets all around. Terror squirmed under my skin. The pipe beside me looked like an angry mouth full of creatures waiting to crawl out and chew my bones. The slime along the walls seemed to breathe like a great dark throat, like being swallowed into the belly of a snake. Even the trees above glared down menacingly, mocking my torment, pointing at me with long needled fingers. All I could think about was of all the shouldn't-haves. Shouldn't have stayed this long out, shouldn't have been late those other time,s so if I was late, they would worry and not be mad, shouldn't have given Vince the bottle so he wouldn't have smashed it and we wouldn't have had to hide, shouldn't have jumped so many times on the board and broken it, and shouldn't have gotten myself here in the first place, shouldn't have, shouldn't have.

I punched the wall in frustration, adding another ache to my predicament. There was nothing that was going to come and save me, nothing that could be used to pull myself out. The insects seemed to be growing more and more restless, hungry, I couldn't help but to assume. Soon they would gather together and attack me I was certain, soon the unknown dangers of the pipe opening would crawl out, soon the fading light above would be completely gone. As bad as it was, I felt in my heart it would become much, much worse.

I had known only a handful of emotions by this time in my life: sadness, loneliness, homesickness, being scared of bullies and monsters and an array of uncontrollable excitements and joys. Those emotions had been pushed further than my mind could understand during this experience. Now something new stirred within me, the fight for survival. I had not known this fire inside me but yet there it burst, its flames flushing my face and grinding hotly my teeth. I thrust myself against the sides, my fingernails scraping against the thick greasy surface, trying frantically digging, wanting to rip and tear through the concrete and into the earth itself. I kicked against the sides, my chest smacked against the walls; furiously I searched for any leeway, any dent or crack I could find. My fingers scraped every inch. In one frenzied jump and grasp, my fingers sunk into the side.

I grabbed it with my other hand and felt a small grooved ledge which had laid hidden in the dark. I pulled myself up, sliding my left hand up until I found another. There I found the footholds that led up and out of the manhole I had fallen in. I gripped the small holds with all the strength in my fingers, my feet sliding and kicking for support. I fell but immediately jumped up again in the same space, clutching the ledges and hoisting my body upwards in grim determination. Soon I had raised myself enough to wedge a foot into the first notch. This took a lot of pressure from shaking arms but I reached higher, climbing slowly up the grimy and terrible wall.

I had reached the mouth of the hole and grabbed the rooted ground outside. The air was fresher, the smell of leaves and pine washed into my nose. I crawled out on my belly, silent tears slid down my cheeks. I stood up and brushed myself off the best I could, but my body was still streaked with smelly smudges of black, brown and the thickening crimson of blood. I looked behind and the hole stared back with an unblinking eye, it wanted to reach out and swallow me again. I backed away slowly and out of the patch of trees. The sun was well on its way to the other side of the world. Night was feeding off the remains of the day.

I felt completely exhausted and everything hurt. I couldn't run. I felt smaller than before. Something felt broken inside. Being left behind like that while trapped had changed me and the way I viewed the world now. My eyes had even changed, staring at that darkness. I limped through the broken glass of the back parking lot, not taking the shortcut through yards. I turned the corner, staying on the sidewalk, watching each of my steps very carefully, down the hill and back home. The houses seemed to stare at me in disappointment. The street, cooling from the passing of the day, felt indifferent against my feet. I remember knocking on the door and my mom answered as I started to cry again, but this time it was weary, for there was not much energy left in me at all.

I didn't tell her what had happened. She could see I was hurt and dirty but I couldn't tell about the board that broke, the fall, and the hole, Vince leaving me, the insects, the process of my escape, none of it. I never told anyone. Perhaps I feared no one would believe me or would be too angry with me at the time. Or maybe it was all just too much to even comprehend.

It wasn't the last time I would ever fall into a hole. It wasn't the last time I would be swallowed up by darkness and the feeling of impossible helplessness. It wasn't the last time someone would leave me.

Down the path the holes would continue to smack their darkened lips, hidden along the unsuspecting ground, waiting for feet guided by sky lost eyes.

That first fall wasn't the worst fall either. Some of the holes were deeper and had no conceivable foot hold out. Some holes I dug with my own ignorant hands. Some holes I deserved while some I truly believe I did not. Some hurt way stronger and way longer after it was over. And picking up speed through the years I found myself jumping again, reaching new heights each year that would past, changing my reach from trees to stars, leaping above the land higher, soaring above the mountains, tasting clouds and each stumble or fall became harder than ever before.

It was that first fall that began to change me. It opened a gate to new nightmares. It opened doors to new dreams. It changed the speed of my stride. It trained my eyes to look closer. Though it gave me the first true lesson in fear, it lit a fire in me that still smolders, forty years later and no matter how much I have left it unattended, ignored, even doused, it still glows when I lose sight of the light, it still shines when I lose the direction of up. It still burns when the walls are closing in, the darkness blinds and deafens me and it feels as if I may never make it out again.

And though its memory isn't as clear as it once was, either from the years it was shoved under the pillows of my mind or by the slow erosion of time, two essential truths that I learned stay with me today: be wary of magical boards in a forest and never forget that no matter how dark it looks, you can pull yourself up.

Forty plus Summers later I find myself walking outside in these recent bright days where heat once again is burning away the hopes of clouds and the sun once again rules the sky, searing the land and lighting the blue into another opaque oblivion. These days I find myself within the restraints of the requirements of adulthood and due to weary eyes, I cannot step outside without sunglasses. Like many afternoons, after work I take a walk with my daughter, bare foot along the scorching sidewalks taking the occasional shade under the shade of Oak and Palm. This is our time to talk and share stories. She has heard most of mine and I am just starting to hear hers. We talk about struggles and fears and hopes and the possibility of pulling ourselves through. She has so many adventures ahead of her and I am both frightened and excited for her. We turn the corner and lose track of the time, the skies mellow in their luminosity and the sunset of many tomorrows hover hungrily upon the horizon.

WHILE ON A WALK AFTER THE INTERNET WENT OUT

BY ALEX GURTIS

We spotted Craig by a stop sign on Virginia Avenue, the correct social distance two lanes of traffic apart. He rapped his knuckles against the tin stop sign as if he were a bucket drummer summoning us to story time. A generation older than us, our Diogenes from the West Coast yelled across the street at us about how a naked woman with a rat in her mouth chased a car through Skid Row, and how his mother-in-law is trading tamales for toilet paper while he kicks back beers in Orlando, hiding from the virus and his wife. Our laughter attracted a portly man wearing a Darth Vader mask. The shirtless man broke the social bubble we had carefully constructed, his arm waving scattering us like the fall leaves, which Floridians always talked about, but never saw.

AUTUMN ABROAD

Kyoto, Japan

by Emma Guernsey

As an American walking down the streets of American cities, is there old architecture I pass or traditional garb I could don that I could be proud of? Are there any versions of these that don't carry with them a shameful and violent history?
Are there any old songs I can sing?

In Kyoto I finally experienced "fall" as the verb, not just as the noun stating the time of year or as the adjective describing a new cafe menu. I knew why it was called "fall" and I knew that at some point the leaves went from the branches of the trees to the ground, of course.

It still shocked me. The falling of the leaves was constant.

I suddenly envied those who get to walk on this thick orange carpet every year.

I picked up some leaves and put them safely in a pocket. I hoped to press them in a book and maybe display them in a small glass frame one day. However, by the time I got home they were already shriveled and browned. They practically crumbled to dust in my hand.

It made me realize that sometimes beauty isn't ours to keep,

only to behold.

ESTHER

BY AARON MORRISON

Esther leads Michael, who, after two weeks, finally convinces her to help him escape the cell in her parent's basement.

Slipping past the village watch, they enter the forest. Movement is slow since Esther forgot to steal shoes for Michael, though she retrieved the thing Michael calls a "phone."

Esther turns right, and gets far ahead of Michael, who cries in pain and betrayal as a cudgel strikes his head.

"For Agoroth! For the village!" shouts the bird masked woman who slits Michael's throat, then turns to Esther.

"What does Agoroth desire above all?"

Esther forces out her answer.

"Despair."

THE BONNIE AND CLYDE DEATH CAR

BY DARRYL PICKETT

Transcribed from a 1972 tape recording of an interview with Audra Tillman

St. Augustine - June 1954

He had the face of a genteel Mephistopheles, a pointed but neatly trimmed beard and mustache set beneath speckled green eyes. Before I could speak, he trapped me with a smile that would've tempted any Eve in any garden you might name. I never had a white man look at me like that before. I fell, God help me. I fell hard.

A bullet had torn into his left shoulder, and lodged itself near his collarbone. I gave him the anesthesia and told him to count backwards from a hundred. "I never guessed my angel of mercy would be so pretty," he said. Then that smile, and he was asleep.

I was nineteen that year, part of a team of four nursing students, all young black women, at St. Agnes Hospital and Training School. My mother was Etta Tillman, an advisor for St. Augustine's College. She had been a nurse with the Red Cross during the war. She was a pioneer, and I was expected to live up to her example. She started training me to be a nurse when I was just four years old.

Our patient was named Eli Corbin, according to his license. Twenty-five, but he looked older, like he'd been already through two or three lifetimes of trouble.

Once the bullet was removed, I helped the other students with the sutures and stitched up two incisions on his neck and shoulder. I had seen far worse. Etta Tillman didn't raise me to be squeamish.

Eli Corbin was the talk of St. Agnes Hospital, the dashing caucasian patient in ward 3A. We saw a lot of matinee idols in the movies, but didn't meet many in our shielded academic community.

Professor Bailey assigned me to watch him during recovery, along with two other students. He mostly talked to me, no matter who was attending to him. Professor Bailey thought she might have to reassign me, as I was distracting him so much. I didn't ask for any of it. But I guess it showed that I was enjoying it.

I was in the room when the Professor said to him, "We're looking into getting you reassigned to another hospital."

"Why? I'm fine here. Or am I the wrong color …"

"We just want to make sure that you're comfortable," Professor Bailey said officiously, then walked out, leaving unsaid how unusual and disruptive his presence had become.

"I'm very comfortable," he said, smiling. Then he turned to me. "I can see that *you're* not."

I didn't say anything, I didn't need to. He was reading me like the morning paper.

"If it helps at all, I'm not as white as I look. I got ancestors from Cuba, from the Seminoles, and even a splash or two of black in my blood thanks to my plantation-owning grandparents. Not ashamed, nor am I proud. It's just how I got here. Can't change that."

"We've had white patients before. You're younger than most we see here. You might even be running from serious trouble. That's what the girls think, Mr. Corbin."

"I can't wait 'til you start calling me Eli. And I'm more trouble than you can imagine."

I was beguiled. I could have fainted at his smile. "That's the problem right there," I said, trying my best to appear unfazed. "You act like you're trying to get under my skin. It's a distraction to the other students. And me."

"I don't mean to distract others. Just you."

Overcome by an impulse, I kissed him. And did he ever kiss me back. I never knew who I was until that kiss. We left the hospital together late that night. I never returned.

*****

Eli was an advance man for the Sowers Brothers traveling carnival. He made sure all the right people were paid off before the show came to town. No doubt his biggest asset was his easy charm and good looks. But it got him into trouble. The only reason he wound up at St. Agnes school was that a cop didn't take his bribe, and chased him to our end of town, shooting him in the shoulder before Eli lost him.

I don't know why Eli took to me. He could have chosen anyone. He was a conman, and I was his mark. I walked into it with my eyes wide open. I accept full responsibility for the damage it did to my reputation, my mama's reputation, the school's. I know what I did. I would do it all again. I wish I could!

Two weeks later, we were in St. Pete, catching up with a show out of Gibtown.

*****

St. Petersburg, July 1954

You're not invited to be a carny. You're either born into it, or you find yourself on the run. Maybe you got a lot of money to launder. The rigged games are perfect for that. Eli was well known, and nobody asked about the young black woman showing him. Not at first.

Near the end of the month, Sowers Brothers booked a charity carnival near St. Pete. Eli was running a lowdown tent show, pickled punks, deformed babies preserved in jars. Didn't bother me. I had seen a lot of medical specimens at the college.

> **" I don't know why Eli took to me. He could have chosen anyone. He was a conman, and I was his mark. I walked into it with my eyes wide open.**

"It's tawdry, and mostly, people are kind of sorry after they've seen it. They wish they'd spent their money on something else." He smiled. "But that won't be the case with what we're about to create, you and I. People will come back. They'll bring friends. It can't lose."

He had been working on this idea since before I ever met him. He was like a kid on Christmas morning when he talked about it.

When the carnival wound down for the night, he led me to a lot near the church. There sat a car, old and unremarkable.

"It's perfect! A Ford Model 40 B. 1934. Still has the original leather seats, in nice condition. It's black, but we could paint it olive green so it matches the original. And we'll have to get a license plate for it. 587-956, Must have been Louisiana plates, and we have to make 'em look old."

"Why would anyone pay good money to see that?"

"Bonnie and Clyde, that's why! It's just about the most famous car in the USA, or at least, everybody's gonna think it is. Bonnie and Clyde's last getaway car, the one they died in. I saw it at a show in Montgomery. Folks paid a dollar just to sit in it, a little more to have their picture taken with it. They lined up for hours."

"Was it the real one?"

"Maybe it was. But then I met a guy who was operating a concession in Miami. He had a fake one that did just as well. People just gotta get close to it. Deep down, people are morbid as hell. It's a powerful combination. Sex. Glamour. Death. You can't go broke, as long as you ignore that righteous angel hollerin' in your ear."

"Don't you need it to look all shot up?"

"Takin' care of that later tonight. We got some guys back at the church who already removed the engine. They're gonna take it out in a field and unload their guns into it. Then they'll replace the engine. We'll have it loaded onto one of the carnival trucks to get it to the next show. It'll. Be a sensation. You'll see. The mark's are gonna thank us."

And I just stared at him, awestruck at the pure shamelessness of it. "The way you talk, you're almost a saint for giving them what they want."

"I understand if you're having second thoughts. People see us carny folk as low. Disreputable."

"They've been saying that about people like me for a long time."

*****

He put his arm around me and we wandered back to the church. He kissed my forehead, and for a moment, I thought we had found a place where we could be together without fear. I should have known better.

"That you, Eli?" said a man emerging from around the corner of the church holding a shotgun, casting a shadow in the harsh security light on the side of the wooden building.

"We were just out in the lot," Eli said, as easy and carefree as always. "I was showing her my prize. Can't wait to get it fixed up."

"You know this woman?" The man was burly, and spoke like a cop does when he's about to bust you.

"This is my secretary. Her name's …"

"Lorna," I said, impulsively. "Lorna Davis."

"You travelin' with the show?"

"Yes, sir. I'm new to it."

The man respected Eli enough to try to hide his disgust for me. "You got an eye for young women, Eli. But you might wanna be careful …"

"She's going to be my wife. The time's coming soon when we can walk as proud as any couple."

"You know where you are …"

"I'm not saying it'll happen *here*. I know what kind of church this is, what kind of vestments your congregation wears."

"Ain't you afraid?" He held his shotgun a little higher, making it clear that we should be.

"I don't have time to worry about being afraid," said Eli. "I got a lot of associates, I can do a lot of favors. Business is good. Don't you agree?"

Eli could charm his way out of danger, but the man needed to intimidate somebody. He turned his attention and his gun on me.

"An' you. You telling me *you* ain't afraid?"

"Every day of my life," I said. "But you're the one who decides if you're gonna pull that trigger. Nothing I can do about it."

He looked back at Eli. "You best take her back to the carnival, let her wait there while we get the Ford shot up. Wouldn't want a stray bullet to hit her, now, would we."

An hour later, five men unloaded round after round of bullets into the body of the car. I could hear it from our tent. I knew Eli was firing some of the shots. I knew at least one of his associates was wishing I was there in the front seat, bleeding.

We got married, in the eyes of the show if not the law. Late that night, after the show had closed and the lights of the midway had gone out, the ferris wheel lights came back on. Eli and I sat in one of the gondolas, and the show boss stood across from us on the loading platform. Not many of the carnies came out to see it, but we recited some vows Eli had come up with. Then the two of us rode that wheel for twenty rotations, nice and slow, so Eli could kiss the bride all he wanted. It wasn't something we could have done in the eyes of the law, but it was just possible in the shadow world of the show, even in a place that was hostile to the idea. Anything is possible when you accept that you will always be on the outside.

*****

Orlando, Late July and August, 1954

We opened our new attraction at the Central Florida Fair, one of the biggest shows of the year, right on the shore of Lake Eola in the middle of Orlando, Florida. Our lot was at the back end of the midway, where the sideshow tents, human oddities, and burlesque revues held sway. I was at my ease here in the fairground equivalent of the slums. I fit right in. The manager of the striptease even tried to get me to join his show. I told him I was flattered, but Eli and I were gonna be the hit of the show.

I was right. The Bonnie and Clyde Death Car was a sensation. The night we opened, it was almost as if our tent had a gravitational pull. As the evening went on, the brighter enticements at the front emptied out, and we were thronged. The taboo is always alluring, but this was thrilling. Old money walked in next to new money, tailored Italian suits followed after department store specials. I saw fine diamonds and ostentatious costume jewelry, rugged jeans and farmers' daughter skirts, all walking in together. I took their money, and Eli took their pictures. They could stand near the car, or for an extra charge, they could sit inside of it, on top of the titillating blood stains. If they had their own camera, they could take a picture free of charge. And if they wanted to tip us, we didn't say no. Eli spun a story about how we came to have the car, and every time he told it, it got more spellbinding, if not more absurd.

So many people surrounded our tent, I was afraid the ground beneath us would crack and we'd tip over and slide into the lake. The carny roughnecks and the Fire Marshall put up barricades and told everyone on the outside of it that they'd have to go home. After a few nights, they moved us to the front end of the midway. We got our share of complaints, but those voices were drowned out by the sound of coins dropping in our till. The police, the Fire Marshall, the city council, and the show officials got their cut. At the end of the first week, we had about enough to get us through the rest of the month. Takes money to make money. Eli knew it well, and I was learning.

Oh, Etta Tillman, you warned me I would find myself in bondage. But instead I found happiness. I found freedom.

*****

I chose to live among thieves. They accepted us. Me and Eli weren't a scandal to them. I didn't have to pretend to be someone else. Did I become a criminal? I still can't exactly answer that. In the eyes of the law, I was born a criminal. So what difference would it make? My mother wanted me to become respectable by becoming as much like polite society as I could, but they will only allow us to get so close and no further. It seemed more honest to live this life.

But that decision carries risk. With popularity comes scrutiny. I knew in my gut we would be raided, and we were, with only three days left of the fair. We didn't run a rigged game, we gave people exactly what we said we would, except that it wasn't the actual car. We were targeted, plain and simple. The warrant cited forgery and fraud, like that wasn't every tip on the midway.

At least 50 armed officers set up barricades around our pitch. They charged into the tent and dismantled it. They grabbed our cash drawer, our books, everything. A fat deputy pushed me to the ground, put his knee on my back, yanked my arms around and cuffed my wrists, wrenching them so tight my hands went numb.

I was hauled up and shoved into the back of a squad car. The cop hollered in my ear that I was under arrest. I was laid down in the back seat, out of sight as they drove me to the station. I was hustled into an interrogation room, then left by myself for at least an hour. Eventually, a senior detective and a young officer came and sat across from me.

"I'm sorry if my boys were a little rough on you," said the older detective. "You're Audra Tillman, daughter of Etta Tillman."

"She's been lookin' for you," said the younger man. He said it like I ought to be glad. I was lost and I had been found. "You're momma's on her way from St. Augustine. We aren't pressing charges."

"Then I'm not under arrest?"

"Technically, but nobody's pressing charges," said the gruff older man.

"Then could you take off these cuffs. I can't feel my hands."

"I'm not authorized to do that yet. I just got to ask you a few questions, then you'll be free to go. The man you're workin' for, he's a wanted criminal. You help us out, I can guarantee you'll walk out of here free."

Like that was something I could do. Going back to St. Agnes would be bondage, no matter how much I loved my sisters there, no matter how I admired my mother. It was that or betray Eli. I knew he would tell me to do the latter.

"What do you need to know?"

*****

Etta Tillman arrived at the station just as the sun was starting to set. She was dressed in her finest gown, gold and red, with matching scarf and clutch. She was caught in a ray of dusky sunlight as she came through the station door. She was radiant, the heroine came to save her wayward daughter. The younger detective whistled in disbelief at the sight of her.

"You didn't tell us you was from wealth."

"We ain't," I answered, but he didn't hear. I knew it was her Sunday finest, bought on layaway at Montgomery Ward. But she had decided to make the best possible impression on any authorities she had to talk to or deal with.

When she saw me, she put on the look of stern but caring admonishment that always came when she knew she had won. I had always given in, and thanked her for showing me the error of my ways. But this time, I knew I was right, and her road was never gonna be mine.

"I'm sorry, Momma."

She extended her arms, ready to give a reassuring embrace. I wasn't ready to accept it. And I didn't have time to think about it. Two rough looking men were holding open the front door of the station, and outside, a car approached. "Audra!," shouted Eli, from the driver's seat of the Ford Model 40. My knight had arrived.

An alarm from inside the station began clanging. My mother jumped in shock, and her arms flew to her head, her body crouching defensively. "Audra," she shouted, and it was the last thing I ever heard her say, the last I ever saw of her.

They say that time stretches at those decisive moments. I had less than a split second to decide to bolt for the car and Eli, no time to think about it. It was as if some force pulled me to the door. I felt hands at my shoulders as I moved, officers trying to restrain me. I propelled myself through the door and down the steps, one after the other, each a springboard. One of the carnies had opened the passenger door, and I sailed through it.

Eli's hand come down on my head as he floored the accelerator. "Stay down," he shouted, but my feet were still hanging out the door as we peeled away. Gunshots sounded from the station. Two struck the open door shattering the passenger window.

Once we were around the corner, I had time to pull myself all the way into the car and shut the door. "Don't sit up," Eli said. "They aren't gonna stop shooting. We're not free yet."

I was seated, but slid down so that I was out of sight. I saw the top of the Orlando downtown buildings, lit up as the night fell. I saw at least one red light as we sailed past it. And I heard the sound of sirens not far behind us.

"It's not a big city," Eli said. "There's a lot of farmland nearby. We can lose 'em pretty quick."

We reached one of the rural highways, and turned off on a random dirt road. With our headlights off, I could see the stars and a bright quarter moon. Eli ran the car off the dirt path and into a soft patch of grass. After about half a mile, he shut off the engine.

"If the grass hides our tracks, and we stay quiet, they're gonna have a hard time finding us." He rolled down the window and leaned out. We both held our breath, hearing only the din of insects, thousands of them, cloaking our presence with the scraping and chirping of their wings. Eli shifted the Ford into neutral.

"I'm gonna get out and push, see if we can maybe get to those trees, stay out of sight."

Eli got out. I started to open my door. "You stay inside," he called out. "Keep an eye out for me."

He was strong. Soon enough, the car inched forward. I was surprised as we picked up speed, like we were on a downward slope.

My rush of hope and excitement flipped to dread when Eli shouted, "Audra, get out of the car!"

The next few minutes seemed to happen in slow motion. The back of the car went up in the air, and the front end plunged down. The earth opened up and began swallowing the car, with me in it. The hood hit water, and if I didn't get out, I was going to drown. I slid through the open window and struggled to climb up and out.

At the same time, a hundred yards away, came the strobe of police lights, the glare of headlights, the wail of sirens. They had found us already. They had been waiting for the right moment to launch an attack.

The car lurched beneath my feet as they opened fire. More bullets hit the death car, and at least one of them hit Eli. I screamed his name as my feet met with the spare tire on the back of the Ford. I jumped off of it just as Eli fell, and I caught him in my arms. He and I hit the ground together.

The police had stopped firing and came running, their voices accompanied by at least ten flashlight beams as they ran toward us. I dragged Eli to the trees. He opened his mouth to scream, but I hushed him.

The cops got to the sinkhole in time to watch the last of the death car sink into the water. They started firing rounds into the hole, hoping to kill us in case we hadn't drowned. If they had trained their lights just a few yards to the left, they might have seen me pulling Eli behind the wooded copse.

Eli was gasping, and bleeding from his right side. He managed to whisper. "I think I can walk. Let's get some distance before they figure out where we are."

"Hold on," I answered, as the flashlights began to spread the range of their search.

I helped him to his feet. I had managed to keep my jacket on and my purse around my shoulder. I pulled off the jacket and wrapped it around his waist. He leaned his full weight on my shoulder, his face twisted in a grimace of unbearable pain. "I'll try not to bleed too much. Don't want to give them a trail to follow." He tried to smile. Even in that desperate moment, he wanted to make me smile, to reassure me with his confidence and charm. Is there anyone who doesn't see why I fell for him so hard?

We found a farm on the other side of trees. It was a modest wooden barn and an even humbler shack house next to it. I could see the rows of crops on the opposite side. A lot of corn, okra, and tomatoes are grown out here.

I set Eli down next to a wooden fence and ran to the front door. I rapped softly but urgently at the door of the shack. An old black man answered the door presently. He didn't need to ask me anything. I just told him why I was there. "The police shot my husband. He's bleeding."

The old man understood and followed me to the fence. "Let's get him inside," he said quietly. "My wife won't be any too happy 'bout it, but don't let that worry you."

"His name's Eli Corbin. They'll be coming around looking for us."

"My name is Coleman Ames," he said, but his eyes told me a lot more. He knew this white man was my intimate partner. We were on the run from the law. He was going to help us. Maybe we weren't the first people to seek help here.

We were able to carry Eli into the house. It was mostly one room, with a small closet and washroom at one end and a door to the fields at the back. His wife sat awake in bed at the other end of the room. She looked like my grandma, which was comforting and daunting at the same time.

"Coleman, who are these people!" she whispered harshly.

"They need help, Bernice. This man is dying."

"He gotta do it here?"

I moved over to the bed and spoke directly to her. "I'm from St. Agnes nursing school. I got to take the bullet out and try to save him."

"They'll be comin' to the door. Nowhere to hide you in here."

I turned to Coleman. "Help me get him out back to the fields. I can try to do something while we hide there. Just tell them you haven't seen us. Please."

Coleman helped me get Eli out the back door, I had a needle and surgical thread in my purse. He offered me a small but clean knife. It was the best he could do. "I gotta go back in the house. Try to make your way into the corn patch, stay out of sight."

I thanked him and urged Eli a few more steps. I set him on the ground and tried to make a comfortable place for him to lie down. "I have to make an incision," I told him. "No anesthesia."

"Won't matter. Pain is already so bad, I probably won't even feel the knife."

"It might get infected. Nothing I can do about that. If there were some way to get you to the hospital."

"I'd rather die than let them catch me. I got a longer rap sheet than you know about."

"Quiet now," I said, and got to work. I removed his shirt. The wound was bad. I found the bullet easily enough. I extracted it with my fingers, using the knife to get at it, trying not to make the entry wound worse than it was.

He lifted his right hand and took hold of the bullet as I removed it. He held it up in the moonlight. "You hang on to this," he said and handed it back to me. "Might be worth something." He smiled, a tired and defeated smile, but still sly and beguiling.

I had to stop the bleeding. But the more I looked, the more I realized what Eli already knew. I had training as a nurse. He needed a surgeon, and a highly skilled one at that. The bullet had torn through muscle and veins. He was bleeding out, and there was nothing I could do about it.

"Leave me here. Let them find me. Get away while you can."

"I'm not leaving you, Eli." I rested my head on his shoulder and wept, as quietly as I could. He took hold of my hand, and we spoke no further.

I saw the lights as a squad car drove up the dirt road to the shack, heard two officers get out and start talking to Coleman. I couldn't hear their words, but I know that Coleman and Bernice denied having seen anyone. I could tell that the officers entered their house, but they never came out back. I felt Eli's chest still moving haltingly beneath my head. His grip was getting weaker.

By the time the cops drove off, Eli had slipped away. I held his hand and rested my head on his chest for another minute or two. Coleman walked out to me. He didn't need to ask. It was clear that I had lost my patient.

"You're covered in blood. We gotta find something for you to wear, and get you out of here."

I nodded my head, unable to form words.

"They got a couple of officers trying to go down in the water, see if they can find anyone or recover anything. They probably gonna give up soon enough. A sinkhole is a dangerous place. You got time to get cleaned up, and we can decide what to do with this man."

Back in the house, Bernice helped me clean up. She fought through her disdain for my choice to make Eli my husband, and out of respect, told me she was sorry about his death. "It will always be like this," she said.

Late that night, with the police long gone, we put Eli's body into the back of Coleman's pickup truck, wrapped in an old blanket and rolled in a rug. Under cover of darkness, Coleman drove me back to the fairground.

"I don't know if they'll try to retrieve your car. What are they gonna find if they do?" Coleman asked.

I explained the nature of the car, and why it was covered in bullet holes. As to what might be inside, I told him. "They already confiscated all our money, the records of all our transactions over the last two weeks. Our camera and film. Nothing criminal about any of that. But I'll never see any of it again."

"You gonna bury this man?"

"I'm hoping the show boss will know a way to do just that, somewhere he won't be found."

"I'm a criminal too. Bernice don't like it. I do my best to lay low. A lot of folks don't want us here. I'll pray for you. It's about all I can do for ya. If you're ever out this way again, my door is always open."

By then, we were at the show entrance by Lake Eola. The lot was dark but the usual late night drinking and card games continued. Somebody went and woke up the show boss. Coleman helped get Eli out of the back of his truck, and then rode away. News of my reappearance spread fast.

At four in the morning, the carousel lights were turned on. Nearly the entire show community turned out for Eli's funeral. He was set on one of the carriages and the carousel was set in motion, backwards. It was a solemn ceremony, and quiet, but for the whirring of the motors. The calliope was shut off, and there was soft singing among those assembled. Beautiful Dreamer. They sang roughly, in different keys, but it was the most beautiful music I had ever heard.

Quietly, the show boss said to me, "That car was the biggest sensation we ever had. We're gonna give Eli the finest burial we can. Leave it to me."

I left the next morning on a bus for Gibsonton. The show would return there soon. So would Eli.

*****

The Ames Farm, 1959

Five years later, I returned to Coleman Ames' farm. He and Bernice were dead by then, but the farm had passed to their son Carter. He had been able to expand the fields and build two new barns. The sinkhole had become a modest lake, and children had turned it into a swimming hole, complete with tire swing. I was shown one of the the newer barns. To my amazement, the car was there, under a tarp. It was rusted, battered and bruised. "We got it out about a year ago. I didn't want to kids jumping in and hurtin' themselves on it. I can have it hauled away unless for some reason you want it."

I told him I had come for exactly that. And it turned out Eli had one surprise left for me. "We found this in the trunk," Carter said as he handed our old cash box. "We haven't opened it. But whatever is in it is probably ruined. There were three guns as well. They're no good anymore."

Eli had stolen them, and had retrieved the cash box before he bravely drove to the police station. He was ready to defend the two of us if we had gotten to safety. He was foolhardy and reckless, and it cost him his life. I told Carter I wanted it all.

The cash box held three-thousand dollars of water-damaged cash. I managed to rescue fifteen hundred of that, ironed out and cleaned up. After all, I worked with the best cash laundry there ever was.

I stayed with the Sowers Brothers for several years and traveled with them all along the Gulf coast, up into Georgia and Alabama, all over. I learned the life, and made myself useful and respectable to people everyone else saw as suspect and disreputable. I was treated without prejudice in this shadow society. Polite society is still trying to catch up.

Epilogue: Jacksonville, 1972

I own a roadside gas station and a little museum outside of Jacksonville. I have a little girl to care for. Her daddy is still traveling with the show, and I never hear from him. I named my daughter Eliza Corbin Tillman.

Inside my little museum, the Bonnie and Clyde Death Car has found a permanent home, alongside numerous oddities and artifacts I picked up over the years. The car is the star attraction of my modest little tourist trap, though. It's not much to look at. I never tried to repaint it or gussy it up. It's rusty, dented, a roadside wreck. I had a new sign painted that looks just like the sign Eli and I had in our show so long ago. The Bonnie and Clyde Death Car! On a couple of small plaques is written an account of the sensational exhibit that got raided and the showman who was hunted down. People who ask can get me to tell the whole story if they want to hear it. I have cases displaying the rusted guns, the cash box, and the bullet that took Eli's life.

I let everybody know about how we faked the real getaway car. A lot of people don't believe me, though. They think it's the real thing, not in spite of its poor condition, but because of it. They still want to think Bonnie and Clyde died on those very seats. They still need to feel the connection, the danger, the romance.

Of course, it has all of that, but not because of Mr. Barrow or Miss Parker. It's because of Eli and Audra. It's not much but it's all the legacy I need. And the money is going to give Eliza opportunities that I either didn't have, or defiantly threw away.

I threw it away for love, the reckless, doomed kind of love that I had could only have found with Eli. Would I wish that for Eliza as well? As her mother, no. I don't want her to go through that much pain and hardship. I don't want her to have to live in shadows. I don't want her to know fear.

But what love! Oh my God, what love I knew.

BACKHOUSE AND GIBBES

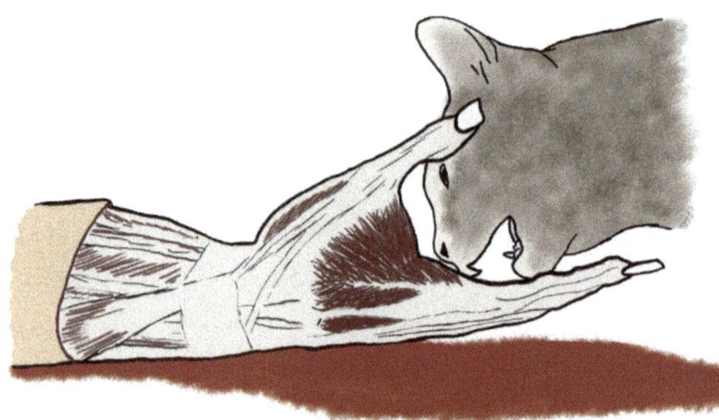

BY AARON MORRISON

"God damn you, Horace Backhouse!"

Conor Gibbes slammed his fist down, rattling the laptop on the desk. He stood and began to pace the length of the study. He ran a hand through his slicked back hair and tugged at his goatee.

"What is it?" Eleanor did not look up from her book. Her unconcerned blue eyes continued to move from line to line.

"Backhouse!" Gibbes exclaimed again, as if that explained everything. "He beat me out for the Barker Jackson award. Again!"

"You'll get 'em next year."

"Gah!" Gibbes waved his hand, dismissing Eleanor's comment. "This rivalry has taken more than its pound of flesh."

"He's won five awards to your one," Eleanor noted. "Hardly a rivalry."

"I have to find a way to defeat him," Gibbes continued, completely ignoring Eleanor's comment. "If not in skill, perhaps in spirit. If I could cast his will to write to the four winds, and sow salt on his inspiration, that would be the way. Yes. Yes."

Eleanor looked up from her book.

"Well," Eleanor said, as she closed her book, setting it down on the end table next to her chair. "I'm going to take a bath and head to bed. Perhaps you should join me." Eleanor stood, touched Gibbes on the back and kissed his cheek.

"I'll join you soon enough," Gibbes responded. He contorted his lips in a subtle kissing motion toward Eleanor that missed its mark by far. "I must sort this devil out."

"Well, don't take too long," she replied. "You know how you get when you don't sleep."

"Yes, yes."

Eleanor left the study.

Gibbes continued to pace around the room, hands crossed behind his back.

"How?" Gibbes muttered. "How can I rid myself of this accursed affliction? I must break his spirit, just as he has broken mine."

Gibbes scanned the room and looked for some clue to aid in his remedy. His eyes fell upon the books on the shelves. Titles jumped out at him.

The Haunting of Manor Hall.

Rats! Rats! Rats!

The Phantom Swamper.

Gibbes stopped his pacing.

"That's it." A devilish grin grew on his face. "I will become a phantom. A ghost to haunt him. I will permeate his mind and torment him, as he has done to me! To break his will to write will be the sweetest of ambrosias, and a balm to soothe my nettled soul." He clapped his hands together and strode out of the study in triumph.

~~~

The swish-swoosh of Horace Backhouse's corduroy pants filled the space between his utterances of "hmm" as he walked. A waif of a man, he
~~~

scampered about, full of nervous energy. A driving cap covered the mop of brown hair that adorned his head. A gray, wool vest completed the ensemble over his flannel print shirt.

His house was dimly lit, and burst at the seams with vintage and antique goods. Old china cabinets full of half empty liquor bottles. Bookcases stuffed with various tomes. Tin toys sat alongside blades of ritual importance from every continent.

Backhouse picked up one of the many mason jars he had not so strategically placed around his home. He twisted off the lid, sniffing at the contents.

"Hmm," he uttered in curiosity, and took a hearty drink of the fermenting liquid. His cough was followed by an oddly pleased smile. Backhouse twisted the lid back on the jar and looked down at the cats meowing at his feet. "Magellan! Caleco! Where is the rest of the Brood?"

The two cats meowed in response before they skittered off to find their brethren.

Backhouse continued to wander about his home.

Skritch skritch skritch

He cocked his head at the sound.

Skritch skritch skritch

"Rats, perhaps?" Backhouse mused. "If so, the Brood will get them. Though the stench will be unbearable should they leave their little corpses in the ceiling and the walls. Oh well." He shrugged. "Will cross that bridge should it arrive."

Backhouse finally found himself in his bedroom. He sat on the edge of his bed and selected one of three mason jars that sat on the nightstand next to the bed. Two gulps later, Backhouse fell back on the bed, barely getting the lid screwed back on the jar in time.

~~~

"Backhouse."

A deep and distorted voice called out.

"Backhouse."

The author's eyes fluttered open.
~~~

"Backhouse."

He pushed himself up slightly with his left elbow to look for the source of the voice.

Just beyond the doorway stood a figure in the darkened hall, adorned in a black hooded cloak. A face, white and featureless, peered out from the folds of the hood.

Backhouse looked down at the mason jar, still held loosely in his hand, and then back up at the phantom that stood before him. He blinked, but neither the figure, nor the haze of his stupor, went away.

"Who... who are you?" Backhouse whispered.

"A phantom sprung from the very depths of your being," the figure responded.

"What do you want, Phantom?" Backhouse inquired, his voice still not much above a whisper.

"Perfection, Backhouse," the figure answered. "I am a reflection of you. A spectre born from the spaces between your ingenuity. Here to haunt you until you are rid of me."

"And how shall I be rid of you?"

"Seal me away with flawless prose, or starve me by ceasing to create the void on which I feed."

The figure then receded into the darkness and disappeared.

"Hmm. Hmm." Backhouse looked about and tapped an anxious finger against the mason jar. He sat up, took another drink, then stood and stumbled to his laptop.

~~~

For weeks it went on.

Backhouse drank more and more from the various jars.

He didn't eat.

What little sleep he received came when he lost consciousness from his now almost permanent stupor. When he awoke again, he would rise, drink, and write some more.

The Phantom scratched at the walls, alternating between mocking Backhouse and egging him on.
~~~

After a month, Backhouse finished his book.

~~~

Gibbes pushed away from the desk and flung his hands up into the
air. He stomped over to the leather chair on the other side of the study
and flopped down. He placed his right hand over his face, dark circles
beneath his eyes. He flung his left arm over the chair in the most dramatic
fashion.

"What is it?" Eleanor asked without looking up from her book.

"Read!" Gibbes stretched the word and raised his arm just enough to
point at the computer.

Eleanor sighed, set down her book, and walked over to the desk.

"'Horace Backhouse's latest work, The Tulpa in My Walls, is nothing
short of a landmark of writing. As if by some magic, Backhouse seamlessly
flows between traditional prose, poetry, and stream of consciousness,
proving he is a modern literary master. He has captured the internal
and external struggles of the creative process in a way never before seen
in literature. A transcendent experience, Backhouse has created a work
that is both deeply personal, yet universal. A perfect blend of horror
and introspection, The Tulpa in My Walls will sit among the greats as
essential reading for generations to come.'"

Gibbes, hand still over his face, shook his head. Eleanor settled back
into her chair, and picked up her book.

"How could this happen?" Gibbes muttered. "I sought to be his
tormentor. Instead, I became his muse."

"Don't you think this has gone too far?" Eleanor turned a page.

"Too far?" Gibbes lifted his hand enough to look at Eleanor. He
scrunched his nose as if he smelled the most foul of scents. He looked
away and began to massage his temples. "No. No. Of course! It wasn't far
enough. I only pushed him to the brink of madness. The place where all
great artists dwell. I led him to that beautiful and terrible precipice, and
hoped he would fall over the edge on his own. All I had to do was push a
little harder," he flicked his fingers out, his thumb still resting against his
forehead, "and he would have plunged into that darkest canyon."
~~~

Eleanor briefly looked up at Gibbes.

"Why don't you start focusing on your own writing again?"

"How?" Gibbes retorted. "I could no more move the block in my way than Sisyphus could reach the top of the hill. There is no creativity left in these hands." He stretched his arms out and looked at his palms. "No prose left in these fingertips."

Eleanor rolled her eyes and turned another page.

"The last remaining creek of my skill has gone dry." Gibbes sighed as he slowly closed his hands into loose fists.

Silence hung in the study until broken by the turning of a page.

"Of course." Gibbes looked from side to side at nothing in particular. "That has to be it. My abilities have left me at the same rate that his have improved. 'By some magic.' Those relics and rotting books. He found some spell to put on me. Draining my skills like some vampire exsanguinating their victim, nourishing himself at my expense. It all fits."

> **❝ *Backhouse was naught but skin and bone. His hair was unkempt and wild. He shook like a small dog left out in the rain.***

Gibbes shakily pushed himself out of the chair.

"Where are you going?" Eleanor asked.

"To retrieve my inspiration." Gibbes mumbled and shuffled out of the study.

~~~

Clack clack clack!

Gibbes struck the door knocker of Backhouse's front door.

Clack clack clack!

The door finally opened.

"Ah! Mr. Gibbes!" Backhouse greeted him. "Do come inside!"

Backhouse was naught but skin and bone. His hair was unkempt and wild. He shook like a small dog left out in the rain. He stepped back and opened the door wider to let Gibbes enter. Without a word, Gibbes
~~~

stepped into the house. He took a few steps into the foyer and stopped. Backhouse closed the door, and walked past Gibbes. The vapors of some unholy mix of fermented liquids left a trail behind the thin man.

"Come. Come." Backhouse waved for Gibbes to follow.

They entered the cluttered living room, and Backhouse turned toward Gibbes and squinted.

"Have you been sleeping well, Mr. Gibbes?" Backhouse asked. "I mean no insult, but you appear quite ashen." Gibbes slowly shook his head. "Hmm," Backhouse tapped his chin, then turned to the large glass door cabinet. He perused the bottles on the shelves. "Perhaps a bit of brandy... Ah! Here we are." He took a bottle off the shelf and poured two glasses. "This particular brandy was aged in apple wood barrels and mixed with extra hard apple cider. An almost perfect blend of sweet and tart. Ah! I see you've found my book collection."

Gibbes' attention had turned to the set of books on the massive bookshelf. He stared at the collection as he fidgeted with something in his pocket.

"I find it important to read just as much as, if not more than, I write." Backhouse continued to talk as he handed Gibbes a glass. Gibbes mindlessly accepted the brandy.

"I've read all your works, Mr. Gibbes," Backhouse continued. "It's inspiring. You, among all the others on those shelves, have helped foster my own continued desire to write. I find it absolutely invigorating to absorb all that talent and skill, to let my mind marinate in the juices of imagination, allowing the impulses of madness to work their will."

"Absorb?" Gibbes mumbled.

"I must tell you, Mr. Gibbes. Your arrival is most fortuitous." Backhouse took a sip of brandy. "I was just pondering the grand possibilities of collaboration."

"Collaboration?" Gibbes muttered and slowly turned toward Backhouse.

"Think of it, Mr. Gibbes! Working together. Our minds in tandem. Me writing through you, and you writing through me. Imagine the possibilities!"

"Writing through you." Gibbes finally looked directly at Backhouse. "I know my solution." He slowly removed the scalpel he had hidden in his pocket.

"Yes, Mr. Gibbes!" Backhouse raised his glass of brandy in a toast. "It is only in embracing our darkest impulses that we can shed the fetters that keep us from our true potential."

What little light there was in the room glinted off the scalpel in Gibbes' raised hand.

~~~

Magellan, Coleco, and the Brood chirruped and meowed as they licked and nibbled at the exposed muscle of their master. Their content and ignorant purring mingled with the clicking and clacking that came from the man in the corner who typed away.

The gloves and mask, made from the flesh of his former rival, made the physical act of typing awkward at first, but he acclimated quickly. He and the new flesh had become one. He was reinvigorated, and now that he had retrieved his inspiration, he knew this one would be his masterpiece.
~~~